THE THREE SISTERS
&
THE HEALING CROWN

THE THREE SISTERS
&
THE HEALING CROWN

-A novel in the spirit of a Nordic fairytale-

Emily K. Stevens

ISBN: 978-1-947347-09-0

First Edition, 2024

For Michelle and the ending I wanted for you.

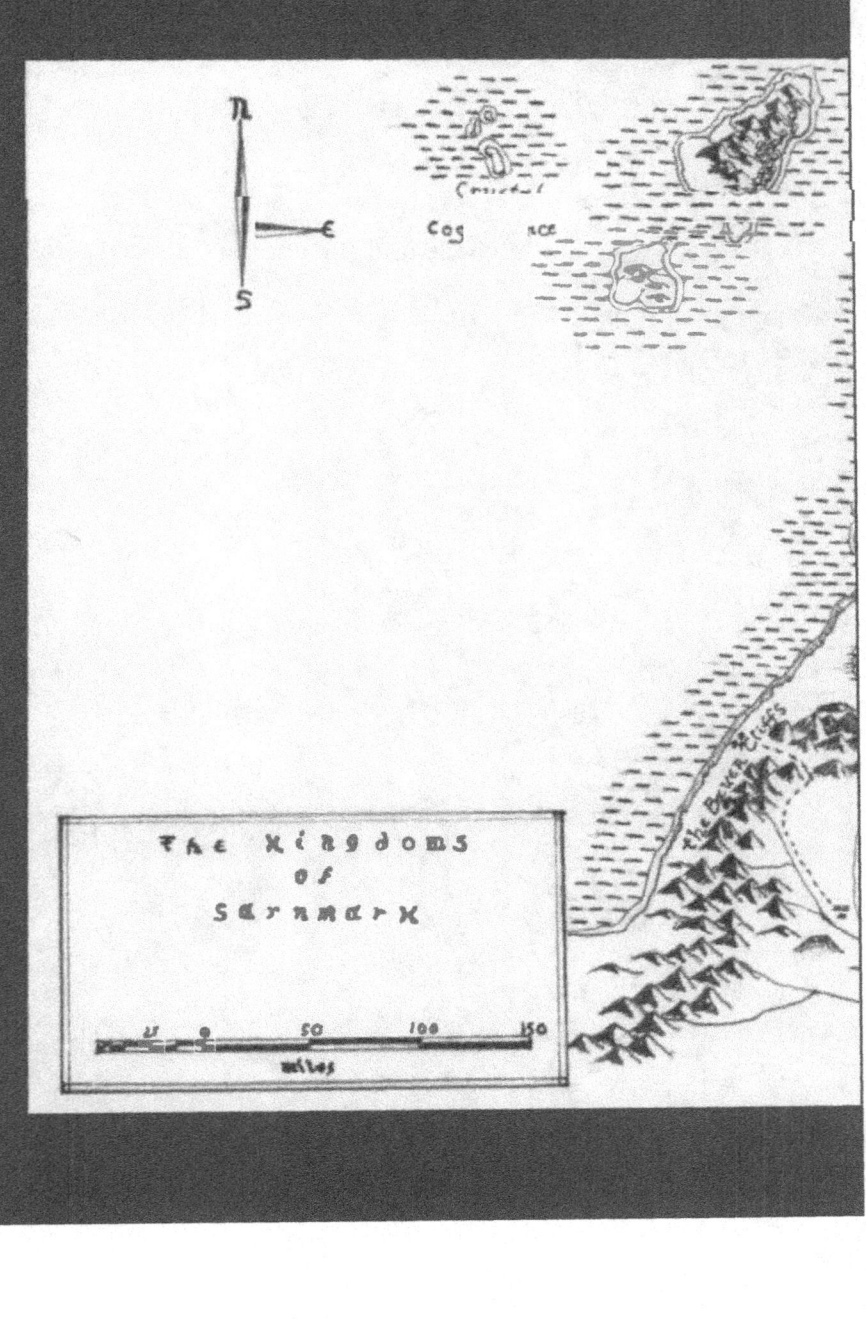

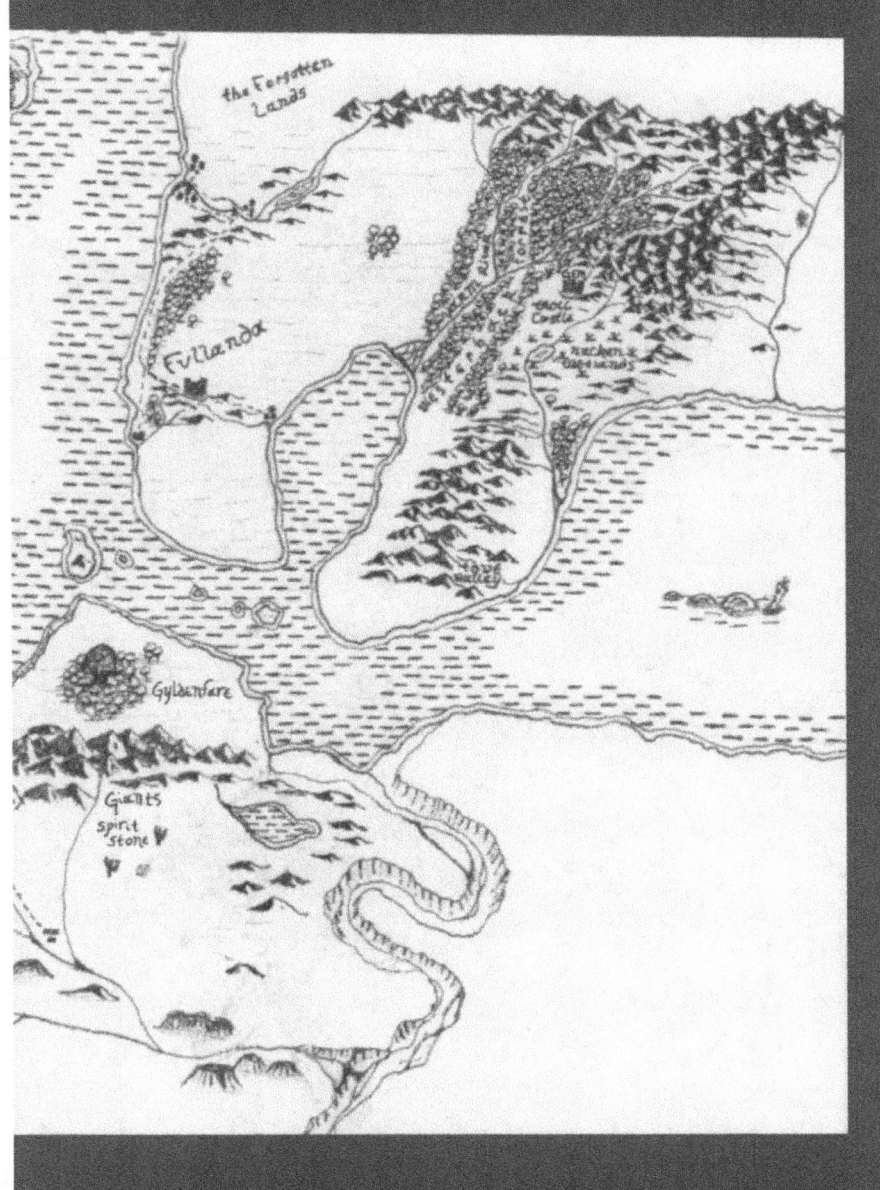

1

A Shadow in the Forest

A shadow drifted through the forest, slipping silently across the floor of pine needles and fern, shunning the late summer sun as it wove its way through the birch trees toward its quarry.

A young woman was dancing alone in a clearing near a meandering stream. Her eyes were closed, but her steps were confident and fluid. Though the air was perfectly still, the woman's long hair and skirts seemed to drift and float, carried by nearly invisible hands. Wind elementals danced with her, their own steps more wild and free.

The shadow narrowed its eyes. "Breezes!" It scoffed. Those elemental ninnies would be no challenge.

The shadow smiled and watched one moment longer, savoring its eminent victory. It then slipped into the stream, reveling in the cool movement across its skin. With a twist of a finger, it summoned its own nature spirits, the water Nixies, to its side.

Swimming against the current, they moved closer to the edge of the clearing where the girl danced on, oblivious to her danger.

She shone like a beacon, bathed in light, her nearly white hair and translucent skin reflecting the sun's rays.

The shadow knew that speed would be its best ally once it left the protection of the shady river. As the girl turned her back, the shadow made its move. It surged through the water, straight towards its prey, flying from the stream on a turbulent wave of Nixies, a look of triumph on its now exposed face.

The girl didn't hesitate in her movement. She merely added a graceful flick of the fingers that sent her attacker flying into a thick pine tree.

"Owww! Was that necessary?!?"

The shadow emerged from the trees and revealed itself to be a girl of about the same age, or, rather, a girl of exactly the same age.

"What happened to sisterly love?" Rania asked as she picked a pinecone out of her wavy blue hair. Everything about her was in shades of blue- hair, eyes, skin and mood- at the moment, anyway. Like water, she was ever changeable.

"You were the one who attacked me," replied Linnea, her ghostly-looking sister. "I told you I'm not in the mood for your games today, Rania. Go pester Sylvi."

"She's too good at hiding and not nearly as easily riled as you are," Rania laughed as she brushed the rest of the pine needles from her clothes. She stopped in the action, her eye catching a movement high in the air.

"His bird is back; Grandfather's bird!"

Linnea stopped dancing and looked up, straining to see in the direction Rania was pointing.

They watched as a majestic gyrfalcon landed on a tumble of moss-covered boulders nestled up to a birch tree. A shiver seemed to run through the rocks as two wood Nymphs broke away, laughing, and ran off into the forest. The remaining rock rolled its shoulders and stretched.

Sylvi resembled her sisters in features, if not coloring. The moss and lichens seemed to vanish from her skin as she faded into her natural light green. She nodded at the gyrfalcon perched on her knee, listening intently.

Rania jogged over and asked, "Is he back already?"

Sylvi looked up. "Yes. They should be arriving in the next hour or so."

She gave the bird a nod of thanks and ran a finger down the back of its head before it sprang into the air and lifted away.

Linnea frowned. "But they've only been gone a week."

"Did that bird say anything else?" Rania pressed.

"Quite a few things, actually, but nothing else concerning Grandfather."

Linnea glanced up the stream. "We better get back. I want to change before they give their report to Grandmother and the court."

"Waste your time if you want to," Rania scoffed. I'm going straight to the stables. They'll have to stop there first."

"Kolbein said that Grandfather wants us to meet him in the library at two- just family."

A silence fell over them, thick with the realization that the news could not be good. Each of them lost in their own thoughts; they followed the stream out of the forest and back up through the formal gardens to the castle they called home.

2

A Mysterious Illness

Sylvi sat on the floor of the library, leaning against the side of a well stuffed chaise lounge. Her mother, Elin, lay there, propped up in a fitful sleep. Sylvi turned a page in her book, listening for changes in her mother's breathing.

They both loved the library, with its vaulted ceiling, stained glass windows and comfortable nooks. They particularly loved all the places the books could take them once her mother could no longer venture from home.

Sylvi tried to remember exactly when she first noticed that her mother was ill; it happened so gradually. A coughing fit when they were running in the field was explained away by all the pollen they had stirred up. The fainting spell at the Midsummer ball was surely just because the room was so warm, but by the time Elin and her fire Imp could no longer make it up the grand staircase without stopping to rest, no one could find excuses anymore.

Sylvi's grandmother, Queen Christina, had sent for all the healers in Fullanda. When they had no explanation, she moved on to the magicians and enchantresses.

When that also failed, she started sending her husband, King Erik, out on longer and longer expeditions, trying to find anyone who could help heal her daughter.

Part of the problem was that Elin had never been ill before. Though a blessing, it emphasized that she was different from regular folk, just as her daughters were. They each had a bond with elemental spirits, which gave them special abilities, but it also made the usual cures and spells act differently on them.

The door to the library clicked, and Sylvi's head popped up. It was her Grandmother. For a moment, Sylvi wondered if she had conjured her with her thoughts. Jumping to her feet, bare as usual, she quietly padded across the room towards her regal matriarch.

"How is she doing?" The Queen asked in a hushed voice.

"I haven't been here long, but her sleep has been less fitful, I think."

"Your Grandfather should be here soon, and the apothecary. Do you know if she's taken the last draughts he sent up?"

"She has," said Elin's soft voice from the couch, "just like a good little girl, even though they were foul beyond belief. What does he put in those things?"

Sylvi rushed to her mother's side, followed by the Queen at a statelier pace.

"How are you, Mother?" Sylvi asked.

"A bit better," she said, mustering a smile for her daughter.

"You need to be eating more, Elin," the Queen barged in. "How do you expect to get better if you don't eat anything? Sylvi, go to the kitchens and have them make up some fresh broth."

"Mother, stop- I don't need...," but Elin's sentence was interrupted by a coughing fit.

Sylvi ran to a nearby table and poured a glass of water. As she handed it to her mother, the door opened.

Sylvi sighed with relief as her grandfather walked in, but the feeling froze in her heart when she saw the look on his face. Her grandmother must have seen it, too, thought Sylvi, as she watched her usually rigid shoulders sink.

Tall and assertive with windblown hair and sun-stained skin, Erik looked more like a sea captain than a king. He inclined his head briefly towards his wife as he walked directly to his daughter and knelt at her side. He produced a small bouquet of wildflowers and presented them to her.

Elin smiled as she took them, giving him a kiss on the cheek.

"How's my little one?" he asked in a voice just for her.

"Oh, Papa, even *my* little ones aren't little anymore. How was your journey?"

Sylvi hadn't noticed the small group that came in after her grandfather until an impatient Rania blurted, "Were you able to find the woman? Can she do something for us?"

Linnea, descending from the balcony, tsked at her sister, "Don't be so rude, Rania. Let Grandfather speak."

The king sighed and stood to address the whole group. "It's fine. It's not a long story and is quickly told. We found the wise woman three days ago. She was very heart-sick and apologetic, but as we feared, there is nothing she can do."

The Queen's eyes flashed. "Nothing she *can* do or nothing she *will* do?" she asked with a tone that suggested which she believed to be true.

"Now, Christina...," started the King, but she cut him off.

"I refuse to believe it!" the Queen fumed as she paced before the fireplace. "I am sure that woman could have helped us if she really wanted to. She got us into this mess. Did you offer her the jewels?"

"You do her an injustice, Mother," said Elin, trying to sit up. "I'm sure that offering payment would have offended her, and this isn't her fault."

"She wouldn't take the jewels," the King said, "and Elin is right, my dear. I am convinced she *would* have helped us if it was at all in her power."

A silence seemed to thicken in the room as the true meaning of the news sunk in. It was Sylvi who broke the silence.

"What about the crown?"

"What crown?" Linnea cut her off sharply.

Rania rolled her eyes. "Tell me you're not talking about that healing crown again. It's broken, Sylvi! You know that."

"The crown isn't broken," Sylvi muttered. "Its magical healing powers don't work because the stones were removed years ago so they could be returned to the kingdoms that loaned them to us, but I... I wasn't talking about its healing powers."

"It's *alleged* healing powers," Rania added under her breath.

Linnea was more direct in her criticism. "Is there any evidence at all that it ever actually worked, even when it had all of its stones?"

"Girls, please," their mother cut in with a tired voice. "Let your sister speak. Go on, darling, I'm listening."

Sylvi, who had retreated into the shadows, cleared her throat and started again.

"Well, it's just that the enchanted moonstone, the one at the center of the crown, stayed here because it's the power stone of Fullanda. It has always been here. It's supposed to have the ability to suspend life- not indefinitely, but it might give us some time."

"Some time to do what, exactly?!?" Linnea asked skeptically.

The Queen and Sylvi's simultaneous answers clashed in the air.

"To find a cure."

"To find the stones."

Linnea couldn't believe that her sister would retreat into faerie tales at a time like this and was about to tell her so when she saw her grandfather's hand raised in a call for silence. With a subtle tick of his head, they all turned their attention to Elin, who had closed her eyes and was clearly getting weaker by the moment.

"Sylvi is right," he said, putting every ounce of calm he could muster into his voice. "The moonstone was used that way in the past, but there is a danger. The wearer's illness is suspended because they fall into an enchanted sleep that lasts for seven weeks and seven days."

"Isn't that just eight weeks?" Rania mumbled under her breath.

Linnea, the only one close enough to hear her, elbowed her in the ribs without a flicker on the attentive face she had turned to their grandfather.

"At the end of that time," the king continued, "the sleeper must be awakened, or they will remain asleep forever."

The Queen looked determined. "Eight weeks should be ample time to find a more powerful wise woman or enchantress. The moonstone protected Fullanda for generations before that ill-fated experiment with the other power stones. It will protect my Elin until we can bring her a cure."

"And at the same time," added the King, "I can set out to hunt down the other stones."

Hands on hips, the Queen turned towards her husband.

"Erik, we have discussed this. It makes no sense to waste time on a dangerous and futile quest."

"I've been researching it for years, Christina. I know where the stones are now. It's not a futile quest."

The Queen's nostrils flared. "I need you to lead the search for the cure. You're the only one who knows the territories between Fullanda and the Forgotten Lands."

A small cough drew their attention, and they all turned to see Elin smiling weakly. "Do I have any say in this?" she asked.

Without waiting for a response, she went on. "I'm tired. I welcome the rest that the moonstone can give, but please, whatever you do, don't take *any* unnecessary risks on my account. I don't regret the choice that led to this, but I couldn't bear it if anyone was hurt or lost because of me."

"Wait, what choice...," Rania began, but the Queen cut her off.

"The crown is in the private vault. I'll need your help collecting it, Erik. Keep your mother company, girls, but don't pester her with unnecessary questions."

She gave each of them a hard stare to let them know she was serious and left the room only once they had all nodded.

3

Three Perfect Rose Buds

Elin smiled at her daughters and motioned for them to join her. Rania and Linnea nestled in on either side of her as Sylvi sat back on the floor and rested her head on her mother's lap. Elin's hand lay palm up. It seemed to glow with a faint, reddish light.

As if drawn by the sight, a fire Imp slowly emerged from the fireplace and stood behind Elin. It put a gentle hand on her shoulder and closed its eyes as it swayed gently back and forth.

Linnea blanched at how dim her mother's elemental was. It looked like a light breeze could put it out.

Elin placed her glowing hand over the flickering fingers on her shoulder and sighed. "I think we both need some rest, my friend. Sylvi, will you help her to the fire and tuck her in with that fat birch log I see at the top of the pile?"

Rania hurried over and grabbed the log as Sylvi helped the Imp back to the hearth. It brightened a bit as the papery bark started to kindle.

"Oh, my girls," Elin said, beckoning them back to her, "I remember when I was not much older than you are now, and all I wanted in the world was to have a child."

"And then you had three," put in Linnea, looking horrified.

"And then I had three," smiled Elin, "which was a triple miracle since I had been told by an old wizard that I could never conceive a child."

The girls knew the story well, so Rania supplied the next line. "Devastated, you ran into the woods and got lost."

"I wandered for hours before an old woman with a goat appeared on the path and asked if she could help me find my way. As we walked, she told me that I should never believe old wizards and that the young ones were even less reliable, and that if I really wanted to have a child all I needed to do was find a silver cup."

"With two handles," Sylvi put in.

"With two handles," nodded their mother, "and place it under a lingonberry bush at the next full moon. Then I was to whisper my heart's desire to the air, water and earth. In the morning, I would see if the powers of nature were willing to aid me."

"So you did as she instructed," Linnea prompted when it looked like their mother was starting to doze off.

"Yes, and in the morning the cup held three perfect rose buds. I knew from the woman's instructions that I was supposed to eat what I found in the cup. They were so delicious I ate them all up, and nine months later, you three miracles were born, and my life was changed forever."

She smiled wistfully and looked at them each in turn. "I love you all so much. Please be good to each other while I'm... resting."

The girls smiled back, but as their mother's eyes closed, the calm slid from their faces.

None of them had noticed when the queen and king had returned, but they now came up behind their reclining daughter and gently placed a golden crown with an iridescent moonstone at its center upon her head.

Elin's breathing became even, and the creases in her forehead slowly released as she slipped into an enchanted sleep.

4

A Message in the Moonlight

A shadow stalked through the dark castle hallways. It was cold, but it was on the hunt for knowledge, and the one person who could quench its thirst was not tucked up in bed like a good little princess should be at this hour.

At that thought, Rania laughed. She wasn't tucked up in bed, either, but everyone knew that she was not a good little princess. That was Linnea. She would be queen one day, so she took her role as princess very seriously.

Rania enjoyed reminding her of what a wild child she had been. The two of them used to be thick as thieves, coming up with schemes and pranks, climbing trees and rolling down hills. Linnea used to love playing the Shadow Beast game. They used to take turns being the shadow and stalking each other.

When their mother became ill, Linnea started shadowing their grandmother instead, and Rania became a lone shade, left to wander on her own.

She could always get Sylvi to play, but if Linnea was the good *princess*, Sylvi was the good *girl*, or rather, good person. Rania had no idea how Sylvi could behave all the time and sit still during lessons, but it was for this very trait that Rania sought her out now.

Why wasn't she in bed? It was almost midnight. Then it struck her- Sylvi had been the one to take on most of their mother's care in the last few months. Rania changed direction and headed down the stone passageway leading to the library.

A dim light shone from under the big oak door. It creaked as she opened it.

Sure enough, Sylvi's head popped up at the sound. She was sitting in her usual spot on the floor with her back against Mother's chaise.

Rania was distracted by how her mother seemed to give off a faint light in the dark vastness of the library. She looked serene yet unearthly-untouchable.

As Sylvi closed her book, Rania's attention was drawn back to her sister.

"Why aren't you in bed?" she asked her.

"I couldn't sleep. What about you?"

Rania came over to sit next to Sylvi as she replied. "Me either. I keep thinking about..."

"What mother meant by the 'choice' that led to this?" Linnea said from behind them, causing Rania to jump and Sylvi to drop her book.

"Where did you come from?" Rania demanded, angry that she hadn't known she was being followed.

"Sometimes even shadows have shadows," Linnea replied with a rather self-satisfied grin.

"What's that supposed to mean?" Rania asked grumpily.

"I saw the light from your lantern under my bedroom door and followed you. What took you so long to find Sylvi? She's always in the library."

Rania won a hard-fought internal battle not to punch her sister in the arm.

"I've been wondering what mother meant, too," said Sylvi. "Does she know what caused her illness? Why wouldn't they tell us?"

"And what else aren't they telling us?" Linnea added as she joined them on the floor. "Grandmother must already know because she didn't seem shocked or dismissive at mother's words. She just told us not to bug her about it."

"Threatened is more like," Rania amended. "I hate when she gives us that stare. Makes me feel like a five-year-old who stole cookies."

"And Grandfather, too," added Sylvi. "He just looked sad, not surprised at what she said."

A tap at the window made them all jump. Rania scolded herself internally. Shadows don't flinch, and this was twice in five minutes. She scowled when she saw what had made the noise.

"It's Grandfather's hawk. It's tapping on the window. What's it doing here at this time of night?"

"Let it in and find out," said Linnea.

Rania scowled at her sister before getting up and heading to the window, Sylvi following close behind.

"He's not a hawk, Rania, you know that. He's a gyrfalcon, and nobody *owns* him. His name is Kolbein, and he's his own bird."

Linnea rolled her eyes behind Sylvi's back.

"There's something tied to its leg!" Rania said.

As she moved to untie the small piece of scrolled paper, Kolbein side-stepped away from her and presented his leg to Sylvi.

"That *hawk* is a menace. A spiteful, petty menace," she grumbled under her breath, crossing her arms and plopping down onto the window seat.

"There's a key and a note," said Sylvi, "and Kolbein says it's for us."

Sylvi told the noble bird that they were grateful for his efforts and wished him a good night. As he spread his wings and flew off into the sky, she marveled at the beauty of the light from the full moon reflecting off his silent wings.

"Well...?" Rania demanded.

Sylvi didn't know why Kolbein always made her sister so angry. Couldn't she tell he was only teasing her?

She unrolled the note and read it.

"The Tomte & the Nissa by Gunhild Ingebretsen."

Rania grabbed the tiny note from her sister and turned it over, looking for more of an explanation.

"That's it?" Linnea asked after neither of them offered anything more. "What's that supposed to mean?"

"It's a book," Sylvi explained as she closed and latched the window. "I've got a copy in my room, but I noticed the other day that there's also one down here."

It had struck her as odd since the spine was a different color.

"I saw it when I was looking for first-hand accounts from the time when our great uncles set off on their quests to bring the stones back, so it must be over behind that pillar."

As she pointed towards the darkest area of the room, Linnea shivered.

"Why don't we just go back to your room and look at the copy you have up there?"

A mischievous grin grew across Rania's face. "Are you still afraid of the dark?"

"No, I just don't want to disturb Mother, and I'm getting cold."

"She's in an enchanted sleep," Rania pointed out. "I doubt you *could* disturb her, even if you tried."

"Found it!" Sylvi called out, cutting off the others mid-argument, but as she went to take it off the shelf, she was surprised to find that it wouldn't budge. She tried again and still couldn't slide it out. It wasn't until her sisters joined her with their lanterns, adding to the glow of her own, that she tried pushing it instead. The book slid in just enough to reveal a small keyhole.

"The key, the key, where'd you put it?" asked Rania.

Sylvi dug in all her pockets before finding it and handing it over.

As Rania's excitement grew, so did Linnea's dread.

"Don't open it. We don't know what it will do. We don't know who that note is even from."

Rania turned to her sister and crossed her arms. "It's Grandfather's bird. It must be from him. Right, Sylvi?"

Sylvi's brow furrowed. She couldn't remember Kolbein saying who the note was from. She shook her head.

"He didn't say, but I think you're right. He wouldn't let anyone else ask him to take messages, especially to us. Most people are afraid of him."

Linnea just scowled as Rania placed the key in the lock and turned it. A soft click came from the bookcase as it swung towards them, revealing the dark opening behind. Cool air drifted out, laced with the soft smell of pine.

Rania darted forward, an ecstatic gleam in her eye, but Linnea pulled her back.

"Are you kidding me??? You receive a mysterious note with a key to a hidden passageway, and you're just going to waltz right in?"

"Yeah," Rania replied and started moving towards the opening again.

Linnea stepped in front of her and put a hand on her chest.

"At least check for traps first."

"How can I check for traps if you won't let me near the opening?"

Linnea sighed. "Let me summon a Breeze or two. They can take a look, and any trap would just go through them," but before she could enact her plan they heard the library doors open and muffled voices in heated conversation.

Rania grabbed her sisters and dragged them into the passageway, partially closing the door behind them.

"What did you do that for?" Linnea hissed.

"Shhh! It's our grandparents." Rania said as she lowered the shade on her lantern.

5

A Private Conversation

The door frame pressed into Sylvi's side as they
all crammed in to listen at the sliver of an opening.
She bit her lip and fidgeted as Rania turned out the
remaining lanterns, plunging them into darkness.

Their grandmother's voice was getting closer. "I
know that we don't have much time, Erik, which is
exactly why I don't want you sending anyone off on
some futile and dangerous journey. We need
everyone concentrating their efforts on finding a
cure."

"Why do you think looking for the stones is
futile?" asked their grandfather, turning his wife
towards him. "I've spent years doing research. I
know exactly where they are now."

"It's too dangerous. Nobody who set out to
return the stones to their original kingdoms ever
came back. My grandmother was devastated. She
lost all three of her brothers. Besides, we don't even
know for certain that it was the crown that healed
my grandfather, but we *do* know of the loss and
devastation that came afterward. Those stones are
nothing but trouble."

"Perhaps that's because the promise was
broken when your mother's uncles failed to return
the stones."

The girls couldn't see the look their
grandmother wielded on her husband, but it was

enough to bring him up short. In a softer voice he continued.

"I'm sorry, it's just.... Christina, there's something I didn't tell you." He ran his hands through his hair and leaned against a table. "Something I didn't want to bring up in front of the others. The wise woman said that if Elin is not cured, the girls might... start to decline, as well."

The noise that came from the queen reminded Sylvi of a dog being kicked.

"No," the queen choked out, grabbing her husband's arm for support. "I knew we should never have trusted that woman, and why did Elin have to go and eat all three buds? I was content to listen to the woman's warnings and only eat one. She gave very explicit instructions."

"What?" Rania whispered in a gasp, then grunted when Linnea socked her in the arm. Luckily, the main door to the library opened at that moment, covering any sounds coming from the girls' hiding place.

The captain of the guards entered and bowed to his sovereigns.

"Your Majesties wished to see me?"

"Yes," said the queen, and Sylvi marveled at how quickly she had regained her composure.

"Thank you, Edvard. Set a guard schedule so Princess Elin is not alone at night. Please have them notify me immediately if there is any change in her condition."

"It will not be hard to find volunteers, Your Majesty. The entire regiment would give their lives for the princess."

"Let's hope it doesn't come to that. I want to know she is being looked after. I have nurses ready to tend her, but they won't start until the morning."

The guard nodded and bowed. "I will take the first shift myself if you can wait ten minutes for me to inform my second in command."

As the door shut behind him, the queen turned to her husband.

"Please don't go looking for those stones, Erik. I don't trust anyone else to continue the search for a cure. You can find it. I know you can. I know this is a hard thing I am asking of you, but I can't lose them, Erik, I just can't, and I can't lose you."

As the king wrapped his arms around his wife, Rania shut the secret passageway, closing them inside. Linnea didn't even protest. None of them wanted to hear their grandmother cry or, worse yet, let her know they had been listening.

"We're going to find those stones," said Rania, and it felt like an oath.

6

An Invitation to Adventure

Sylvi's face emerged from the darkness as she lifted the lantern shade.

"It looks like a staircase," she said, the light following her as she began climbing.

"Come back here. We need to look for a latch or another way out," Linnea hissed.

Rania tried lifting the shades on the other lanterns only to find they had gone out. Shrugging her shoulders in the growing dark, she started up the stairs after Sylvi.

Linnea gritted her teeth and followed them.

The worn stone steps rose in a tight spiral. Linnea ran her hand along the cold, smooth wall as she followed the light. She took steady breaths, willing herself to be calm.

All at once, the stairs ended, and she ran into Rania's back.

Linnea could feel the warmth of the room as she nudged her way past her sister. An intricately painted ceramic tiled stove stood to the left of the door. Linnea hurried to it and held out her frigid hands.

"Someone's been here recently," she said, looking around.

Two overstuffed chairs were drawn up companionably by the stove. Sylvi lit the lamp that rested on the table between them. Rania found another on the small mahogany desk directly opposite the door. Neatly rolled maps and scrolls cluttered its surface.

"What is this place?" Linnea asked, still warming her hands.

"I think it's some sort of secret office," Rania said, unrolling a map.

Linea rolled her eyes. "Yes, I'd gathered that, but *why* is there a secret office, and when is the person who uses it going to be back?"

Rania shrugged and unrolled another map while Sylvi looked through the papers on the desk.

"What are you two doing?" Linnea asked, raising her voice. "Don't you know it's rude to rummage through other people's things? I'm leaving."

Rania looked up, daggers in her eyes, "Didn't you hear them? We're going to die if we don't heal Mother, and it looks like that crown might be our only chance. That stupid bird sent us here, which must mean there is more information or a clue...."

"Or a letter?" asked Sylvi, holding up an envelope with their names on it.

Snatching it from her hand and ripping it open, Rania began to read aloud.

"My dear girls, I apologize for all the secrecy. See!" she said, looking at Linnea. "I told you the message was from grandfather."

Linnea took the letter and rapidly scanned the page.

"Oh, please read aloud if you're going to read it," asked Sylvi, "or at least let us see."

The girls crowded around Linnea as Rania picked up where she had left off.

"If you are reading this letter, it means my plans to retrieve the stones have been put on hold. Your grandmother wants to keep danger at bay, but I've seen that danger can find you in your own backyard. In the top right drawer of my desk, you will find a journal with maps and notes on the location of the remaining three stones of power, as well as other items to aide you on your way."

Rania left the letter for her sisters to finish as she rushed to the desk and removed a small wooden chest.

"It's locked," she said, dropping it on the desk. "Does he say where the key is in the letter?"

"No," said Linnea, "just that it's our choice whether or not we want to do this really dangerous thing all on our own."

Rania looked at Sylvi for confirmation.

"That's not exactly what he wrote," Sylvi said. "There are some nice parts about how we are stronger than we know and that he loves us."

"But nothing about a key?" Rania pressed.

Sylvi sighed. "Nothing about a key. You... you don't think it could be the same key as the hidden door, do you?"

"Worth a shot," Rania said, brightening.

Sylvi took the key from her pocket and slid it into the lock. The contents of the chest glowed as Rania slowly opened the lid.

"Whoa," said Sylvi, taking a small step back. "That's a lot of gold."

"These will definitely aide us on our way," remarked Rania as she started sorting the contents of the chest on the desk in front of her.

Linnea's jaw dropped open.

"What are you doing?" she asked.

"Dividing up the treasure; it makes no sense to keep it in one place- much easier to lose that way," Rania said. "I think we should hide the coins in unlikely places, like our hair or shoes or the hems of our skirts, in case we run into bandits."

"Don't put them in your shoes," Sylvi piped up. "You'll get blisters."

"Good point," Rania replied.

"What are you two talking about?" Linnea cut in. "You're not seriously considering doing this, are you?!? We've never been away from home on our own, let alone on a dangerous quest."

Rania stopped sorting and looked at her sister.

"Mother needs us, and you heard what Grandfather said. If we don't find a way to make her better, we could be next. I don't know if I believe in this crown, but I would rather be out in the world trying to save ourselves, than sitting at home hoping someone else does."

"Didn't you hear what Grand*mother* said? We need to use this money and whatever else we can find on the search for a cure. There are many brave knights and adventurers in Fullanda. They can cover more ground than we can and have a far better chance of success than three naive girls."

"Is that how you see us? Really??? You command the winds, and you think of yourself as a naive girl? You don't have to come with me, but I'm setting out now before Grandmother or anyone else can stop me."

"Yes, she does," Sylvi murmured. They had almost forgotten she was there.

"What?" they asked in unison, turning towards her.

"She has to come with us. We all need to go, or there's no point."

"What are you talking about?" Rania asked, hand on hip.

Sylvi held out the journal that had been in the chest with the treasure. The page she showed them had a rough map drawn across both pages.

"This," she said, pointing to a spot roughly in the center of the map, "is Fullanda. There are three stones missing from the crown. If Grandfather is correct, one lies at the bottom of a glacial lake in the middle of a frozen island guarded by a lindworm in the far north." She showed them on the map and went on. "Another is said to be held by the brutal troll who took over Saumlina Castle, which is located in a vast haunted forest, all the way over here," she pointed to a spot on the far east side of the map, "and it says that the last stone is located here, in the city of giants, which is on the southern continent."

Linnea looked directly at Rania as she replied, "Well, that sounds easy enough."

"And we have eight weeks to find them all," Sylvi finished.

Rania shook herself and squared her shoulders.

"Right. We'll *all* have to go. I can calm the seas, Linnea can keep the wind in our sails, and Sylvi can navigate when we're on land. We can do this. Let Grandmother send out as many people as she likes to look for a cure- the more, the better. *This mission is ours.*"

Linnea opened her mouth to protest, but Sylvi put a hand on her arm as if to quiet the arguments she knew were about to spring from her sister's lips.

"Both of you are right- we *are* powerful, but we are also untested. It does Mother no good if we run off and get ourselves killed, but I've been looking through this journal, and Grandfather has it all laid out for us. He's even got a small boat provisioned and ready to go."

"Tell me it's the knor," Rania begged. "It's the most versatile, and we're all used to sailing it."

Sylvi nodded. "And it's moored in a secret boat-house at the bottom of this tower. We should be able to maneuver it out without being seen if we're careful and leave while it's still dark."

Linnea opened her mouth again, but Sylvi was determined to finish.

"And there's one more thing- Rania, is there a small wooden box in the chest?"

Rania dug around and pulled it out.

"Inside are three magic rings. Grandfather says that if you twist one around your finger three times and whisper, 'home', it will take you there. This way, if things get too dangerous, we can come back instantly."

Rania opened the box, put a ring on her finger, and passed the box to Sylvi. After taking a deep breath, she also put a ring on her finger and handed the box to Linnea.

Linnea wanted to grab the box and throw it as far from herself as possible. She wanted to shake her sisters and make them see sense. She wanted to wake up and find out that it was all just a bad dream and her mother was fine, but a small voice inside told her that her sisters were right. They needed to try.

She took the box, but before slipping the ring on her finger, she said, "Alright, I'll go since the two of you wouldn't get to Thorsbrook without me, but I am *not* leaving without changing into something a little more appropriate.",

7

Escape to the Sea

"Where is she?" Rania grumbled for the third time in as many minutes. "We left the library three hours ago. We had everything planned out. How long does it take to pack some clothes and get dressed?"

That's when they saw her. Rania couldn't believe it, even of Linnea. She was dressed in her finest visiting gown. The one with about a hundred buttons all down her sleeves and back.

"Ooh, she looks lovely," said Sylvi.

"For a day at court, maybe. Where does she think we're going?"

Linnea's two large trunks were hoisted along by Breezes, who dropped them unceremoniously on the dock. Rania tried picking up the first one and almost threw out her back.

"What is in this thing?"

"You might not care what you look like, but first impressions are very important. We are the royal family of Fullanda. It is important that we represent our kingdom with pride."

She looked Rania up and down with ill-disguised disgust.

"Is that a dagger in your boot??? What kind of message are you trying to send?"

"That I'm not to be trifled with," Rania replied with a smirk.

Linnea just wrinkled her nose and moved her critical gaze to Sylvi, taking in her bare feet and what seemed to be some sort of beggar's garb.

"And you, what are you supposed to be?"

"I thought I'd blend in if I looked like a boy from a fishing village. Besides, wearing breeches makes it easier to work the sail."

Linnea rolled her eyes. "You're not going to need to work the sail. I told you I would find some Breezes to take us downriver, and when we get to the ocean, the Winds can help us out."

Rania just shook her head as Linnea's Breezes assisted her onto the boat, looking like an empress. She remembered when Linnea used to be fun. When did she get so... clean?

"Well, *Your Majesty*," Rania said with a mockingly formal accent and an elaborate bow, "Could you ask your breezy servants to hoist your two-ton luggage on board? The rest of the 'royal family of Fullanda' is too busy curtsying."

When Linnea ignored her rudeness, Rania was tempted to ask a few Nixies to spit water in her sister's face, but she was anxious to get going. It was already starting to get light. She untied the back of the boat as Sylvi undid the front, and they pushed off, jumping in at the last minute.

Everything looked touched with gold as they maneuvered downriver. The Nixies guided them around the bend and away from the castle. When the trees got thinner and the river widened, Rania put up the sail, and the Breezes pushed them along towards a dazzling sunrise.

Rania's spirit soared. They were off! She wanted to whoop with the joy of it or swim with the Nixies that rushed them along their way. She contented herself with closing her eyes and feeling the wind rush through her hair.

A weight that had been pressing on her chest since their mother became ill seemed to lift, at least a little, as they sped towards an unknown adventure.

A bump jostled her from her reverie.

"What was that?" she asked.

"Sorry," said Sylvi. "I forgot it got rocky this soon."

It took all of them, working in unspoken unison with their elementals, to make it through the next section of river. They had decided it was safest to get to the ocean as quickly as possible to avoid detection, but it made the journey more treacherous.

Sylvi and her Nymphs moved low lying branches and smaller rocks out of their path while Rania directed the Nixies to guide them around larger obstacles, and Linnea kept the Breezes pushing them forward. They were all exhausted when they paused for lunch.

Rania noticed that a weight seemed to have been lifted from her sisters, as well. Sylvi was less skittish, and Linnea was telling jokes. It felt like the 'before' times, when all they had to worry about was getting caught pilfering sweets.

She hadn't realized how much she had missed it- missed them being a trio.

"I have something," said Sylvi.

She knew that it was naive to think that this journey would go smoothly, but a larger dread had been nagging at her. What if they retrieved the stones but arrived home too late?

She took three short, wide bands of leather out of her satchel and handed one to each of her sisters.

"Thanks?" said Linnea, raising an eyebrow.

"They're for counting the days, so we don't lose track of time. Each morning, we make a mark on the leather. I've already marked them for today. We've only got eight weeks, so I thought it was important to keep track."

It was a credit to her sisterly love that Linnea put anything so rough looking on her dainty wrist next to her embroidered cuff.

Rania smiled. "This is great! Thanks, Sylvi."

'Yes," said Linnea, "very clever, but why do we each need one? Couldn't just one of us keep track of the days?"

"But what if one of the bracelets falls off or gets scuffed, and we can't read our markings? I think it's safer if we each have one."

Rania thought she knew what Sylvie was trying very hard not to say. What if one of them was in danger and had to use their ring to get home or, worse yet, was hurt and couldn't twist their ring in time?

It made a chill run down her spine, but she shook it off and fastened the tracker to her wrist.

As they ate, a goose landed in the water near their boat and gracefully paddled towards them. It squawked at Sylvi and ruffled its feathers.

"We better get moving," Sylvi said, tossing bread to the goose and thanking him. "They know we're missing and have started searching."

The rest of the route downriver was less treacherous, but there were several small towns with fishing and trading vessels. They would need to be careful if they didn't want to be recognized.

Though the knor wasn't marked as a royal ship, if any of the elementals were seen helping it downriver, there would be no doubt who was on board.

They packed up what was left of their meal, and Linnea took off her bejeweled over-dress in favor of the more utilitarian dove gray under-frock. She then sent a Breeze ahead as a lookout and returned the rest to the sail.

"Uhhh," groaned Rania. "I wish we could stop in Glomborg and pick up some pastries. They really are the best in the kingdom. Nea, can't you send a Breeze to nab a few?"

Linnea smiled wickedly, clearly liking the idea, but time and secrecy were of the essence, so their afternoon was sadly devoid of pilfered treats.

It was a harrowing day. They thought they had been seen by a fishing boat only to realize that the single passenger was sound asleep, oar in hand.

The last mile was through a section of rapids that had them all sweating with concentration and effort. It was almost disconcerting when they sailed out into the calm of a large bay.

"We did it. We made it to the sea," Sylvi said, stretching her aching back.

"Of course we did!" said Rania.

Even Linnea was smiling, but Sylvi couldn't quite relax. Something was wrong. She listened hard.

Faint splashing noises seemed to be coming from the far side of the inlet.

"Can you hear that?" she asked, quieting her sisters down.

Linnea sent a Breeze to take a look. "It's a seal," she said, "caught in a net."

Almost before the words were out of her mouth, Rania had stripped off her outer garments and dove into the water.

Linnea asked the Breezes to blow the boat after her.

As they neared the commotion Sylvi and Linnea could see that Rania had used her boot dagger to cut the seal out of the net.

"I told you it would be useful!" she yelled from the water.

Linnea motioned for a Breeze to blow a wave over Rania's head.

Rania came back up with a grin on her face. Sylvi knew she had to distract them, or it would turn into an all-out war, and she really wasn't in the mood to get wet.

"The seal is trying to tell me something. Please hush."

She was never as good at communicating with ocean animals as those who lived in the forest, but she gave it a try.

"I think she's hungry? It sounds like she was stuck here for a while. Linnea, grab some of that fish from the barrel."

The seal seemed excited to have someone who could understand her. She spent the next five minutes describing in detail the whole ordeal and became eloquent in praising Rania's prowess as a rescuer.

"What is she saying?" Rania asked.
Sylvi wrinkled her nose and decided to relay a highly edited version.

"It sounds like she wants to follow us, if we don't mind."

"I don't mind if she tags along," Rania replied, "but if Linnea gets one of the winds to help us, it will be hard for a seal to keep up. Does she have a name?"

"I'll ask, but it's really quite rude to demand a name this early in an acquaintance."

Sylvi tried her best to ask politely, but she needn't have worried. The seal was ready to give Rania anything; a name seemed like a great deal in exchange for saving her life.

"Her name is Arh-Shim-Shim-Arh-Arla."

"Yeah, I'm going to call her Simma. Tell her she can come with us if she can keep up."

Rania had the Nixies lift her on board. She shook her head like a dog, a look of elation on her face.

"Alright, Linnea," she said as she started changing into dry clothing, "time to contact the North Wind."

"What???" gasped Linnea, dropping the dried fish she was collecting for the seal. "No, no, no, not the *North* Wind! We talked about this back at the castle. The plan was to go east first, then west, and then ask the South Wind to take us to the North. From there, we can use the rings to get home, so there's no need to encounter the North Wind at all."

Rania frowned. "I've been thinking about that. The North Wind is the fastest, right? If we can catch him on his way home, we could get to the ice island first, before it gets any colder."

Linnea fidgeted in her seat. "He'll be cranky if he's on his way home and worn out from his long journey south. If you want to go to the ice island first, why don't we ask the South Wind to take us? She may not be as strong, but she's much better company."

Rania's scowl deepened. "I think speed is more important than having a good time. Why are you so upset about this?"

"I'm not upset," Linnea flared. "I just think we should stick to the plan."

"Since when have you been a stickler for keeping to a plan?" Rania shot back.

A knowing smile spread across Sylvi's face. "Since she played a practical joke on the North Wind, and now he has a huuuge grudge against her."

"Seriously?" Rania asked, one eyebrow raised. "How can you play a joke on a wind?"

Linnea turned to Sylvi, giving her best imperial scowl, but Sylvi wasn't daunted. "You put pepper in his favorite dessert and then go on a picnic, knowing he can't resist taking it."

"I was sick of not being able to eat krumkake on picnics," Linnea admitted. "It serves him right for thinking he can take whatever he pleases."

Sylvi laughed. "He sneezed for a week straight. Nobody could hang out their washing without it getting blown two towns over."

"Yeah," Linnea smiled, "That *was* a good one."

Rania stared at them, open-mouthed. "How did I miss this?"

"It was when you were off at the hunting lodge with Grandfather two autumns back. I could have sworn we told you."

"Nope," said Rania, staring at her giggling sisters. "OK, I've got an idea. Problem solved- you just apologize and ask if he'll please take us north."

"Oh no!" said Linnea. "I am not going to apologize. He is a pompous, bullying thief. He deserves worse than he got. Besides, there is no reason we can't do it in the order originally discussed."

"Except that the north is getting colder and darker every day," said Rania. "I want as much light and warmth as I can get for trekking across that wasteland."

As if to emphasize Rania's point, the seal leaped out of the water and started barking.

"See," said Rania, "Simma agrees with me."

"I am not taking advice from a seal," said Linnea, arms crossed, "and I don't think we should start our journey with the hardest task. Can't we just start with the Troll to get warmed up?"

"None of the tasks is going to be easy," Sylvi interjected, "and since we don't even know if the North Wind *would* accept an apology, I think we should stick with the original plan and head east. Do you think the West Wind would help blow us there?" she asked Linnea.

"Please don't tell me she's mad at you, too," Rania grumbled.

Linnea ignored her remark and turned to Sylvi. "Show me exactly on the map where we are and where we want to be."

Sylvi dug the journal out of her satchel. "No one has traveled to the castle in years, so the forest has grown up around it. Great Uncle Nils said he came ashore just north of the Varm River and headed inland in a northeasterly direction."

She showed Linnea the map before safely stowing the journal in her satchel.

"I thought nobody who went to return the stones ever came back," said Rania.

"He didn't come back," explained Sylvi. "He traded the stone to the troll in exchange for a captive princess, and her father was so pleased, he gave Uncle Nils half his kingdom and the princess's hand in marriage."

Linnea just stared at her, incredulous. "But Grandmother said they all came to a bad end."

A smile pulled at the corner of Sylvi's mouth. "I think Grandmother believes that having to live in the troll-infested north-east *is* a bad end, even if you do own half a kingdom."

"Fine," said Rania, finally giving in, "can you ask the West Wind to blow us to the Varm River?"

Linnea closed her eyes in concentration, but it didn't take long for her to open them again.

"She's on her way. You might want to hold on to something."

8

A Change in the Air

Linnea laughed as the West Wind caught them. Sylvi had taken her advice and held on to the bench, but Rania thought herself above such things and was now flat on her back, legs flailing in the air.

The small craft sped across the calm sea, leaving their seal companion behind.

The West Wind was indeed excellent company. She could blow them along while telling outrageous stories of the lands she had traveled.

They heard of how bandits were taking over Bauer castle and how the King of Gyldenfare was on the prowl for his *seventh* wife.

A trip that should have taken days was over in a matter of hours. They waved the West Wind goodbye just as the sun was setting.

"I think we should lay anchor here and wait until morning to go ashore," Rania suggested.

They all liked the idea, and Sylvi began hauling the sleeping things out of storage.
"I'm getting sick of rye bread and dried fish already," said Linnea. "Let's dig a bit deeper in the food stores and see what else Grandfather packed."

Rania grabbed a big, round loaf and pulled a piece off to pop in her mouth. "Rye bread is just fine with me."

"I'm just saying, if there's anything more perishable or too heavy to carry, we should eat it tonight."

Sylvi handed Rania a heavy blanket in exchange for some of the bread. They hunkered down between the benches and stared up at the awakening stars.

"It feels like we're floating," Sylvi whispered, nestling in with a sigh.

"We are floating," laughed Rania.

"I meant floating in the air with the stars surrounding us."

"A-haah!" Linnea's bellow made both her sisters jump.

"Don't yell like that," Rania chided. "I thought we were being attacked."

Linnea came out of the store cupboard looking triumphant.

"I found lingonberry jam, a bottle of wine and a brick of chocolate. I think this calls for a celebration."

"These rations need to last us two months," said Sylvi, eyeing the chocolate.

"I'm not saying we should eat it *all*. Besides, I'm not going to carry pots of jam in my pack once we start hiking into the woods tomorrow, and anything could happen to the supplies on board while we are away.

Sylvi giggled. "Yeah, like the North Wind could steal them."

Linnea's brow furrowed. "That arrogant, bullying crybaby cannot take a joke. Don't look shocked. You know how I feel about that pompous blow-hard. I am never going to apologize to him because I am not, in any way, sorry."

Sylvi's face had gone white. She stood up and pointed.

The hairs on the back of Linnea's neck began to rise. She turned slowly, knowing what she would see.

There was the North Wind, horrible in his anger, flanked by a legion of Gales and Gusts.

Linnea faced him down, defiance crackling in her eyes. Was he really so sensitive that he had to bring a gang to intimidate her?

"What do you want?!?" she heard herself yelling into the gathering storm.

With a flick of the wrist, the North Wind set his minions loose. They rattled the stores and tore at the sail.

Linnea's eyes never left his face.

"I'm not afraid of you!" she yelled.

His eyebrow raised, unleashing utter havoc. Sylvi's mouth was moving, but Linnea couldn't hear her through the storm.

The North Wind suddenly broke eye contact and looked over Linnea's shoulder.

She turned just in time to see Sylvi torn from the boat and dragged off into the darkness by a pair of rampaging Gusts.

"Sylvi!" Rania screamed and only paused long enough to yell, "This is your fault!" back at Linnea before jumping off the boat in the direction Sylvi had disappeared.

Linnea's eyes raked the water's surface-searching for her sister. Rania motioned wildly at the Nixies for help, but the storm was too much for them. As Linnea gathered herself to jump, an oar tore from the boat and hit Rania on the head, knocking her back under the water.

Linnea turned to the North Wind. "I'm sorry, I'm sorry. Stop this!" she screamed at the top of her lungs. As the boat lurched, she felt her knees give out and everything went black.

9

The Selkie Queen

The sun prodded at Rania's eyelids. A thin film seemed to be gluing her lashes shut, but a few drowsy blinks were enough to part them. The fluffy white clouds in the blue sky above were moving by at a steady pace, reminding Rania of sheep being chased into a pen. It took her a moment to realize that *she* was the one moving, not them. She was floating on her back- arms and legs motionless; how was she moving so fast? The push of something solid against her foot called her instantly back to full consciousness.

She struggled and turned in the water to find herself face to face with a seal and two excited Nixies. They bumped up against her and sprayed water in the air with joy.

"I'm happy to see you, too," she said, looking at the Nixies, "but what are we doing in the water?"

The seal splashed happily, sending spray into Rania's face.

"Simma?" she asked. The seal seemed pleased to be recognized.

Rania turned in the water, looking for the boat and the beach. All she saw was open ocean and a small island in the distance. Panic started to rise.

"Where... where are we? This isn't the Varm River. Where are my sisters? Where is the boat?"

She continued to turn in the water, trying desperately to get her bearings, but nothing looked familiar.

As her panic grew, small, smooth heads bobbed up to the surface all around them.

Rania found she was caught up in a mass of seals all heading towards the island.

Since getting out of their way seemed futile, Rania allowed herself to be herded along.
As they got close, she could see a rocky shoreline and a dense wooded area beyond.

Crashing waves broke against the rocks. Rania braced for at least one bruising hit, but the Nixies helped guide her ashore safely before retreating to play in the surf.

Most of the seals laid out to sun themselves on the rocks, but the largest of them, a beautiful mottled female, eyed Rania curiously with her penetrating black eyes. A shiver of her speckled skin, and she was no longer a seal but a beautiful, voluptuous woman.

She stood up, tucked her seal skin firmly under her arm, and walked to where Rania stood, looking on in amazement.

As the woman approached, Simma inclined her head in greeting and started barking animatedly.

The woman nodded and barked back in reply. Simma shimmied over to Rania, bumped her nose gently against the girl's knee, then slid back into the water.

"Simma, wait!" Rania called.

The seal popped its head out of the water and barked happily before disappearing under the waves.

Rania looked around wildly.

The woman put out her hand in a welcoming gesture and said, "Your friend believes that we can help each other."

"Who are you?" asked Rania. She had almost said '*What* are you?' but years of living with Sylvi had taught her that most creatures found that question rude.

"I am the Queen of the Selkies. My sisters and I generally don't allow humans on our island, but I gather from the look of your skin that you are not *entirely* human."

Rania had always thought of herself as human, but it was true that she and her mother and sisters didn't quite look like the rest of their grandparents' people.

She chose to push the thought to the back of her mind for now. She had more pressing concerns.
"Where are my sisters? How far are we from the Varm River?"

The Selkie Queen looked around as if more human girls might be hiding in the bushes.

"I do not know. I was not told of sisters. I was only told that you are in need of safe passage to the far north to the island of the Great Lindworm."

That last word pulled Rania out of her blossoming panic. Lindworm- yes, she needed to get there. It was her best shot at finding the others and the stone.

Rania felt for the ring on her finger, choosing to believe that her sisters were safe and that they could use their rings to get home if things got too dangerous.

"Yes, I need to get there. Can you help me?"

10

A Convenient Cliff

Linnea was snuggled up on a puffy, down duvet that was floating through the air. A light breeze ruffled her hair and cooled her face. It was a lovely dream, so when consciousness started creeping towards her, she grasped her cumulus comforter closer and willed the wind to whisk her away.

Consciousness, however, is nearly impossible to outrun. As Linnea slowly opened her tired eyes and stretched out her limbs, her contentment vanished instantaneously. The North Wind was carrying her in his arms.

Her initial instinct to struggle free was checked by the view below. She could barely see the ocean far beneath the clouds.

"Put me down!" she demanded.
"That was my intent," he replied.

Linnea thought she could see a shadow of something flicker across his face. Remorse? Embarrassment? Indigestion?

Whatever it was, it disappeared as he set her down on the top of a great cliff overlooking the sea. As he turned to leave, she grabbed his arm and swung him around.

"So that's it? You attacked my boat, hurt my sisters, and now you're going to dump me in the middle of nowhere without a word of explanation?!?"

He regarded her as a cat might stare at a mouse that has turned to squeak vehemently at it with raised fists. After a moment, he blinked and uttered a simple "Yes." before floating off the cliff and away from her.

She wanted to scream or cry or throw something at him, but before she could decide which, he turned back to her.

"Your sisters are unharmed. You just needed to look for different treasure."

And then he was gone.

"What is that supposed to mean?!?" She yelled after him, knowing full well that he couldn't hear her.

A blur in the distance caught her eye. In a moment, two Breezes wrapped themselves around her in a loving embrace. They slumped against her in exhaustion.

She hugged them gratefully and asked, "Oh, my Breezes, do you know where we are? Was the North Wind telling the truth? Are my sisters alright?"

They shrugged apologetically. Their sole aim had been to follow the North Wind after he had caught Linnea mid-faint. It took all the energy they had just to keep on his trail.

At least they could tell her that the Lord of the Winds had carried her south and east and that they were many, many miles from where they had started.

Linnea's lip began to tremble when a noise behind her triggered an instinctive response.

She had motioned for the Breezes to throw the intruder off the cliff and into the water before she had even looked to see who or what it was.

"Oh my goodness! I am so, so sorry!" she yelled down to the man who had just splashed into the water below.

"I'll find a way to get you back up here. Are you hurt? Can you swim? Oh, good, I see that you can. My sister sneaks up on me like that all the time, so I'm used to just...."

"I don't know how you did that, little girly, but you're going to regret it," drawled a voice from behind her.

Linnea turned to see a large, rough-looking man slapping a cudgel in his hand menacingly.

She breathed a sigh of relief. "Oh, thank goodness."

The man looked taken aback. "I don't think you understand what's about to happen to you, little lady. You should be scared—terrified. We bandits control this wasteland and...."

The bandit found it hard to continue as he flew off the cliff and joined his partner in the water.

Linnea laughed and thanked the Breezes.

"That was fun. I wonder if there are any other baddies to toss off this most convenient cliff."

A quick look around their make-shift camp, however, didn't produce any more ruffians. Tied to a cart filled with what she presumed to be ill-gotten gains was a rather ragged horse. The only other living thing was a lovely blue bird in a golden cage.

"Hmmm," she mused, "I can't be sure *all* of this is stolen; better pay for what I take."

The horse's neigh sounded almost like a snicker.

Linnea smiled. "And what's your name, handsome fella?"

She took an apple from a basket on the cart and fed it to him, stroking his mane. "Oh, right, it's impolite to ask that question so soon in a relationship. Please forgive me for being so forward."

The horse neigh-laughed again and eyed the apple basket hopefully.

Linnea gave him another, and then started filling a saddle bag with provisions from the cart. As she did so, she talked to the Breezes.

"Can you try to find Sylvi and Rania? I need to know that they really are alright. Please tell them I'm alive and I am not abandoning the search. I *will* find them."

The Breezes gave her blustery hugs and headed back in the direction they had come.

Linnea walked back over to the cliff and called down to the men who were climbing up on a small island not far from the shore.

"I'm going to buy some supplies from you. I'm putting the money at the bottom of the apple basket."

They yelled threats and shook their fists at her.

Whistling as she walked back to the camp, she fished a few coins from the pouch attached to her belt and placed them at the bottom of the apple basket before turning back to the saddle bags.

"Better not make them too heavy," she mumbled aloud. A few substitutions and additions later, she hoisted them on her shoulder.

"Now, which way to go?"

She closed her eyes and tried to sense any local Breezes, but it was dead calm.

Years of geography, natural history and diplomacy lessons had not prepared her for this.

"Well, I might as well follow the cliff, just in case I come across anyone else who's in need of a sea bath."

With a deep breath, she fixed a determined look on her face and stepped onto the road.

A horrible ruckus erupted behind her. The horse stomped and neighed and pulled at his rope.

"What? I paid for it all," she argued. "Are you really that attached to the saddle bags?"

Linnea walked back to the cart and took an apple out of the basket.

"You can have this if you calm down and behave yourself."

The horse didn't even bother looking embarrassed at his abrupt change in demeanor. He ate the apple greedily, but stepped in Linnea's way when she started to leave.

"If I give you the remaining apples, will you let me go?"

The horse harrumphed and narrowed his eyes indignantly.

"Do you want me to untie you? That really *is* a good idea. Who knows how long it will be before those two get back up here? You may run out of apples by then and need to go in search of grass."

She untied him, but when she reached out to remove his saddle, he side-stepped away from her.

"Alright, you can keep it," she said, shrugging.

A whistle and a chirp brought her attention back to the cart.

"My goodness, how could I have forgotten you?" she said as she opened the birdcage.

"Your freedom, Miss Chirperine McFeatherbritches."

The bird hopped forward and cocked its head to one side.

"I know that birds don't wear britches. It was meant to be funny."

The bird just cocked its head in the other direction.

"You're awfully picky, whatever your name is. I leave the door open. It is your choice to leave or remain."

She gave the bird an elaborate curtsey and turned to go.

The horse was standing at the path she had chosen, looking back expectantly.

"Do you want to go with me?" she asked.

He took a few steps forward and looked back at her.

"Alright then, I can't say that I'm disappointed to have company, but you're going to have to carry your own apples."

The horse snicker-neighed appreciatively.

"See," Linnea said, looking back at the bird, "Some people appreciate my humor."

Linnea packed a few more things now that she had a traveling companion who could share the load. When she was done, she went back to the cliff. The ruffians had made it to the bank and were trying to climb up the steep slope.

"I'm going to need to take all of the apples," she yelled down to them, "some oats and a blanket, oh, and the horse has decided to come with me. I'll put the money under the bird cage since the apple basket is empty. Thanks!"

The bandits didn't even bother hurling insults, which she found somewhat disappointing.

She loaded the saddlebags onto the horse, adjusted the stirrups and mounted. Her skirts bunched awkwardly around her, but she was grateful for the extra padding.

As she looked back at the camp one last time, the bird flew over and landed on her head.

"Oh, well, that was unexpected. I don't mind you joining us, but you will be in serious trouble if you relieve yourself up there."

The bird didn't make a move to leave, so she clicked for the horse to move forward.

"It occurs to me," she said, patting him on the neck, "that I don't know your name, either."

"Bwrrrt," whickered the horse.

"Bert? That's a good name. I'm Linnea Margareta Gunvor of Fullanda, but you can call me Linnea or just plain Neah."

The bird hopped up and down on her head. "Alright, alright, I'll try another name for you. How does Whistlewing sound?"

The bird pecked at her head.

"Oww! There is no need to get violent. How about Sir Soarington?"

A slightly gentler peck greeted her head for her efforts.

"What about Madame Sharpbeak? That seems appropriate."

The road lay out before them, and Linnea's wild guesses became more flamboyant as they worked their way up the coast.

11

Mysterious Mushrooms

Rushing waves and the call of gulls wound their way through the cocoon of sticks and twigs encasing the drowsy green princess. Sylvi tried to roll and stretch, but found she could only move a few inches in each direction.

Her eyelids popped open, but sight didn't help solve the puzzle of where she was. Sticks, moss and living branches were all woven together to form a protective barrier. It surrounded her so completely that she wasn't sure how she got there, or, more importantly, how she would get back out.

Instinctively, she reached out her mind to her Nymphs before remembering that she had left them on the other side of the ocean since they couldn't bear to be far from their native trees.

Her movement must have awakened her living cage. The branches retracted slowly to create an opening just large enough for her body to fit through.

She laid her palms on the branches and sent grateful thoughts to the flora that had housed her during the night.

Tentatively, she poked her head out of the hole. She was about three feet from the ground. A whole network of bushes and trees had woven together to protect her.

"Thank you," she whispered aloud as she climbed her way down to the forest floor.

She followed the sound of the waves lapping on the shore nearby.

The water weathered stones felt smooth on her bare feet as they shifted beneath her.
She picked her way down the shore and around a bend, calling out for her sisters.

The devastation that met her eyes brought her to her knees. Their beautiful craft lay broken in the shallows, its contents strewn across the rocky beach.

"Rania... Linnea," she gasped, scanning the wreckage for any sign of them.

Sylvi wondered why she wasn't crying or panicking. As she examined that thought, she realized that her overall feeling was that of a brave calm mixed with hopefulness. The stranger thing was that it seemed to be emanating from where her shins rested on the ground.

Gently, she touched her hands to the rocky beach, and they felt it, too- a warm presence trying to reassure her. Images and emotions flashed into her mind, so Sylvi tried sending some back. She closed her eyes and imagined Rania's face, blue and beautiful with her long curling locks. The presence sent back a picture of her on an island surrounded by seals.

Sylvi breathed a sigh of relief to see her alive and unharmed. Emboldened, she sent an image of Linnea's mischievous smile and white hair waving in the Breeze. The presence sent back a picture of her gleefully tossing a man off of a cliff. Sylvi snorted with laughter, and the presence replied with colors and happiness in reply.

"They are safe. Thank you for showing me," Sylvie said aloud.

As she opened her eyes, she noticed that milk-cap mushrooms had grown through the beach rocks and were nestling up to her fingers.

"Are you a... forest spirit?" she asked aloud. The mushrooms moved gently while sending a picture of an immense web of interconnecting threads under the ground that seemed to go on forever.

"Oh, you're simply amazing," she said in awe. Then a thought came to her. "Can you show me a troll?"

She tried to picture the troll, but realizing that she didn't know what this particular troll looked like, she went back to using words.

"He lives at Saumlina Castle at the far end of this forest."

She pictured the map in her head as best as she could remember it, and the mushrooms tickled her skin, sending her images of a troll being served coffee by a princess in a great stone castle.

"Hmmm," Sylvi thought, "I didn't plan on saving a princess, but I guess I can work that in."

12

The Thief, the Selkie & the Fox

Rania said goodbye to the Nixies as she walked onto the pebbled shore. She could see the Selkie's island as a small dot in the vast open sea.

Looking down, she saw that one of the selkies, still in seal form, had followed her. She dropped an exquisite pearl necklace on the shore, barked encouragingly at Rania, and then slipped back into the water.

"The necklace, right; knew I forgot something," she mumbled to herself.

Rania was actually pretty certain she had forgotten a whole lot of somethings in the Selkie Queen's plan. It seemed strange and far-fetched to her, but it was hard to say if people in this part of the world behaved differently than people in Fullanda or if the Selkies didn't spend enough time around humans to understand them.

One thing Rania was fairly certain they were right about- a blue-skinned girl who showed up on a small island without a boat would be suspicious. That's where the necklace came in. Rania put it around her neck and watched her beautiful azure tone drain away from her hands and then her legs. The Selkie Queen had told Rania of the woman who lived on the farm at the top of the hill and how she held one of their sisters there against her will.

"My clan likes to shed our seal skins on warm moonlit nights," she had explained to Rania. "We did not know that the woman had found our island and was lying in wait. As soon as we transformed, she stole a seal skin and rowed her boat back to the human island. When it was time for us to transform back into our seal forms, one of our sisters could not find her skin. She was drawn to it, so we helped her swim to the human island, but we foolishly let her go ashore to search alone. She never came back. We see her from time to time working in the yard, and we know she will never be free until her seal skin is returned to her."

The Selkies had an unnatural fear of the human island, so they asked Rania to find the hidden seal skin and save their sister.

In return, the seals promised her safe passage north and essential information about lindworms. It was a fair deal, but Rania burned to be off finding her sisters. Every delay, every hash mark on her bracelet, reminded her that time was eating away at the days left to save their mother.

"The sooner I save this Selkie, the sooner I can get back on track."

She took a deep breath and started limping up the well-worn path. Looking like she was hurt and not a threat was part of the plan, but Rania knew she was a horrible actor. Visions of not remembering which leg was supposed to be hurt danced in her head as she moved steadily uphill.

As she neared the house, she saw a beautiful Arctic fox sitting on a rock watching her progress with a curious look on its face. She smiled, and it seemed to smile back until a rock narrowly missed hitting its head.

"Shooo! Get away with you, vermin!" a woman screeched as she threw another rock.

The woman was not young, but neither was she old. Her hair was pulled back in tight braids that came together at the nape of her neck. Her body was lean and fierce as she stooped to grab more stones to throw at the fox.

Before she could loose another projectile, she noticed Rania and turned towards her, stone still in hand. All Rania could do was stand there, teetering on the path.

"Who are you? Where'd ya come from, eh? We don't take kindly to beggars in these parts." She growled at Rania. "Barely enough for those who are workin' their fingers to the bone," she mumbled.

Rania tried desperately to remember the cover story the Selkie Queen had given her- something about a shipwreck? She fidgeted with the pearls as her mind raced.

The necklace's beauty caught the woman's eye and ignited her greed. Her demeanor changed immediately, and she cooed, "Don't you worry, Lassie, I nun gunna harm ya." She put the stone down and showed her empty hands to Rania, who was still fumbling for words.

"Why don't you come on up, dearie, and I can get you a drink, and you can tell me all about how you got here."

Rania limped ahead a few steps, and the woman coaxed her on until Rania found herself inside the cottage and face to face with the Selkie girl.

"There you are, Girl!" the woman barked at the selkie maiden.

Rania rankled at her tone.

"We have a guest; poor thing is half drowned and scared out of her wits. Go get her some water, you lazy thing!"

"Oh, no," Rania tried to protest, but the woman would hear none of it.

"Now you just sit down in this nice comfy chair by the window and put that hurt leg up on a stool. Girl! I'm going to go kill a nice fat chicken to feed up our guest. You get the water on for soup and no dawdling!"

"Yes, Miss Ebba," the selkie replied meekly. Ebba grabbed an enormous cleaver and an apron from a peg by the door.

"You just rest up now and pay no mind to Girl; she's a hopeless creature. I'll be back in two shakes."

Rania looked out the window and waited until she could see Ebba entering the chicken coop before she jumped out of her chair and found the selkie in the small kitchen.

"I'm here to get you back to the sea. Your sisters sent me. Where do you think your seal skin might be hidden?"

Rania spoke quickly, trying to get all the information out before Ebba returned.

The selkie's eyes widened. Then she shook her head.

"I'm, I'm sorry. You must be mistaken. I don't have any sisters. I'm a castaway, like you, and Miss Ebba has kindly taken me in, even though I'm more trouble than I'm worth."

Rania was taken aback. Had she gone to the wrong homestead? Was there a selkie down the coast who was waiting to be saved?

The slam of the coop door closing alerted her to Ebba's return.

Rania hastily sat back in the chair and put her leg up on the stool just in time.

Ebba swung open the cottage door as if expecting to catch them at something. She relaxed visibly when she saw Rania sitting in the chair where she had left her.

"Oh, good, you're getting some rest," she said, bringing the bloody cleaver and apron into the kitchen. In an instant she was back, gathering things in the small room beyond the parlor, talking as she bustled about.

"Now, I'm sure you'd like a good soak and wash after your ordeal, so let's get you out of those wet things, and I'll take you out back to the hot spring. That'll help yer hurt leg more than anythin."

Rania allowed herself to be undressed and to have a homespun dressing gown wrapped around her, but when Ebba's busy hands reached towards her necklace, Rania shied away.

"No need to worry, dearie. You keep your baubles, but be sure not to lose them in the spring."

Ebba handed her a cake of soap and a large wooden comb and pushed Rania out the front door.

"Oh no," she said as they passed the coop, "I better go back and let Girl know that the chicken is draining and that I'll do the plucking and gutting after bringing you to the spring."

She hurried back into the house and closed the door behind her. Rania stood feeling naked, wearing a thin dressing gown and clutching her bath things in front of her. A cool breeze played at her hair. It felt lovely, and then it *looked* lovely.

"A Breeze! Oh, no, quick, hide- she's coming back," Rania whispered frantically as Ebba came out of the cottage.

"Here, dearie," Ebba cooed. "I got you a nice cup 'a tea to have with yer bath."

Rania juggled the soap and comb to get a free hand for the tea.

"Be sure to drink it all up. It's got strong healing in it."

The trip up the hill to the hot spring was breathtaking. There weren't many trees on the island, so Rania could see the dramatic rock formations and the sea beyond.

The hot springs were in a secluded little nook, nestled into the rocky slope.

"I'll leave you to your soak. Got to go make sure that girl isn't slacking. We need soup to feed you up."

Ebba was walking away as Rania asked, "What is her name?"

Ebba stopped, turned slowly and eyed her suspiciously. Rania went on, "She called you Miss Ebba, but I didn't catch her name. I'm Sylvi, if I haven't said yet."

Rania wasn't sure what made her give her sister's name. Perhaps it was because Sylvi was always telling them that names have power and that you must be careful asking for others and giving yours away.

Ebba eyed her shrewdly but must have decided it was a harmless question. "She came here without a name or a past. I took her in, or she would 'a starved."

Rania nodded and turned as if she had no real interest in the matter.

Ebba waited a moment before heading down the path towards the homestead.

Rania breathed a sigh of relief and looked around for her sister's Breeze.

"It's safe to come out now," she whispered. When no Breeze appeared, she put the tea and the soap on a rock and lifted her dressing gown to put a toe in the water. It felt heavenly, even if it did give off a faint sulfurous odor. She found a larger rock to sit on and dangled her legs in the water. She was grateful for the comb. Her hair was an almighty mess, and she didn't look forward to untangling it.

As she started the painful job, the Arctic fox appeared on a rock across the spring.

"Oh, hello again," she said in a friendly tone.

"Hello!" replied the fox. "I wouldn't drink that tea if I were you."

13

A Somewhat Rude Non-Stranger

"If I keep following the coast, I'm bound to find a town or fishing village," Linnea babbled to her animal companions.

The horse, Bert, gave the impression of listening attentively while the still unnamed bird stared at Linnea's hair and contemplated using it for a nest.

"Then, I can see if there is a mapmaker in the area who can show me where we are and if we're near any of the stones. I've got this. *We've* got this," she amended, for Bert's benefit.

Linnea's eyes flashed as she urged him into a gallop. She hadn't realized how much she missed horseback riding. All of their daily routines had changed when her mother became ill.

Tramping about the castle grounds with Rania; whole days spent outside with her carefree Breezes, turned into weeks in the audience chamber studying her grandmother's subtle art of negotiation.

As she galloped down the dirt path, not a soul in sight, a trail of etiquette and rules trailed out behind her and was left in the dust.

They stopped for lunch beside a stream. Bert munched happily on a patch of grass as Linnea scarfed down an entire loaf of bread.

The bird eyed her from a rock.

"What am I going to call you, you particular little thing? How about Persnickety Quirkyson?"

The bird turned its back on her.

"Oh, come on. That was a good one, unless it should be Persnickety Quirkys*dotter*? I'll find you a name one of these days."

When they got back on the road, Linnea began to sing. She started with an epic poem she was made to memorize by one of her exasperated tutors, and then moved on to hearty working songs and bawdy alehouse tunes.

Technically, she wasn't allowed in alehouses, but that didn't stop Rania and her from creating elaborate disguises and sneaking in when a good musician or storyteller was in town.

As she sang, it felt like something inside her had cracked open and been set loose.

That night, she unpacked the blanket that still reeked of unwashed bandit and fell instantly to sleep atop the rocky earth.

When the sun rose, she stretched her sore muscles and hung the dew-damp blanket on a tree branch. The air was more turbulent today, so she summoned a few local Breezes to dry it out before re-packing.

Linnea smiled and whistled as she fed Bert an apple and put out bread crumbs for the bird.

They traveled for days without seeing a soul, but just as Linnea began to wonder if she should have packed more food, she saw smoke in the distance.

"Well, it's either a town or a forest fire," she said casually, changing their course towards probable civilization.

Soon, a small farm could be seen on the road ahead. Rania and her companions galloped up only to find it abandoned by all except a few wild geese.

"Hmmm. Maybe they're off at market?"

They got back on the road and quickly reached the outskirts of a prosperous town.

All the buildings looked well maintained and inviting, yet the absence of inhabitants made its quaintness seem sinister.

"Nothing strange here. Nope. What's your bet, Bert? Are all the townsfolk invisible, or did they lose a bet with a giant and have to move to Jotunheim for a year? Maybe they only appear on a full moon or when the sun goes down?"

The bird looked at her over its shoulder, then flew off to find food scraps on the ground outside of a sidewalk café.

"I can't win with you," she remarked, shaking her head.

A movement in a shop window caught her eye. It looked as though a beggar had gotten inside. She dismounted and was about to check the door when she realized it was her reflection.

The dresses in the shop window were encrusted with fine embroidery and yards of richly dyed fabrics.

All of the etiquette, rules and self-consciousness that she had left along the road suddenly caught up and rushed back in.

Tears welled up in her eyes and would have spilled over if a young man hadn't bustled out of the shop next door just at that moment. The second it took him to notice her was enough to straighten her spine and hitch a smile back on her face.

"Excuse me, Sir," she said, "could you tell me where I am? I seem to have lost my way."

The man seemed surprised to see her.

"I thought I was the only one crazy enough to stay in town this late. Come on; let's get to the festival before they do the sweep."

The man rushed along the abandoned streets, beckoning Linnea to follow him. He only relaxed when they passed through a small gate set in a stone wall.

Linnea stared up at the dazzling castle, easily three times the size of the one she grew up in. The man led her along a well-worn path that followed the outside of the castle wall.

"I am so sorry for the rush. I'm not usually this rude, well, not to strangers, anyway."

He looked so serious; Linnea couldn't tell if he was joking. She decided to assume he was.

"Well, let me introduce myself, so we'll no longer be strangers, and you can start being rude to me in earnest. My name is Linnea."

The man laughed, "And you can call me Pahl, because... well, that's my name."

Feeling a bit more at ease, Linnea asked, "Is there a problem in the town? You said something about a 'sweep'?"

Pahl shook his head. "Oh, I'm probably overreacting. Besides, you're not from around here. You would have no way of knowing that the festival is mandatory."

As if on cue, shouts and cheers could be heard in the distance.

"A festival! That makes sense." When Pahl gave her a blank look, she explained, "The horse and I had a bet. We both lost. So, what *is* this festival?"

"Today is the first day of the Glasberg tournament. If you don't mind traveling with a somewhat rude non-stranger, I can show you the way to the tournament grounds."

Linnea was sorely tempted. It had been ages since she'd been to a festival, but she had no time to waste.

"Thank you for the offer, but I really just need to find a mapmaker and some supplies for my journey. Can you point me in the right direction?"

Pahl stared at her for a moment, not sure what to say. "Um, I'm so sorry, but it's the *first* day of the tournament. Nothing will be open again for three days, well, or until someone collects the golden apple, but we all know how likely *that* is." His chuckle led her to believe there was some sort of joke she wasn't in on.

"We do?" she asked.

"Wow, you really aren't from around here, are you? No one *ever* gets the golden apple. It's just an excuse for a three-day celebration. If it's any consolation, *I'm* a map-maker. If you tell me what you're looking for, I will know if I have it in my shop."

Linnea stopped walking. "You're telling me that this tournament will last for three days, and, what, nobody sells anything during that time?"

"Well, there are food vendors at the tournament grounds, so you won't starve, but it's strictly forbidden to open any shop in the town during the festival. Doesn't make much sense to me; people come from all over the world to compete in the tournament. Seems like a good time to sell them things, but the town is locked up for all three days, and everyone tents out at the festival grounds." Linnea could feel the tears starting to prick at her eyes, again, but she beat them back.

"Tell me, why is it so difficult to get the apple? Why does no one succeed?"

"Well, because the hill is just too slippery," he said. Then, remembering she was a foreigner, he elaborated. "In the middle of the tournament grounds, there is a steep hill made entirely of pure white quartz. At the top stands a beautiful tree of jade hung with golden apples. It used to be common for people to try to scale the hill out of greed or desperation or just on a dare. So many people got hurt in the attempt that the king, not this king, of course, one of his ancestors, decided to set aside a day each year when anyone could give it a go. Nobody ever got even close to the top. As I said, the hill is much too steep and far too smooth, but the festival was a big hit and was soon expanded to three days. Later, kings began to offer great prizes to the knight who could reach the highest point on the hill."

Pahl stopped speaking so suddenly that Linnea had to ask, "What's the prize this year?"

Pahl's face darkened, "The hand of the king's youngest daughter in marriage."

Linnea couldn't hide the disgust in her voice, "That's...."

"Barbaric? Backwards? Infuriating? Exactly! Are we living in the dark times? I can't believe he's just selling her off like property, or worse, just giving her away. Astrid deserves so much better than that."

"Like *you*, perhaps?" Linnea asked, hoping she wasn't overstepping her bounds.

Pahl started to splutter. "Me? What? No... no I'm not better. Well, I mean, I *am* better than that lout Prince Gumay, who will most likely win the tourney this year, but I'm not good enough for *her*. No one is."

A sparkle kindled in Linnea's eye. "I think I can help you. I need this tournament to end, and you need to win the princess her freedom."

"But I don't even have a horse," Pahl protested.

"Ah, but I do."

14

An Array of Traveling Companions

Sylvie sat on the beach, throwing smooth, sun-warmed stones into the water.

The shipwreck debris around her had been searched and sorted into neat piles. A heavy pack leaned against a tree, waiting for her to start the journey into the forest.

She knew she should stand up, turn her back on the sea, and start walking towards the troll castle. Instead, she picked up another rock and tossed it. It splashed into the water with a satisfying plunk.

She picked up another and was winding up for the throw when a stray lock of hair blew into her face. She tucked it behind her ear only to have it fly free again a moment later.

Frustration turned to elation as the mischievous Breeze materialized in front of her.

"Linnea!" she cried out, jumping to her feet and looking all around.

The Breeze shook its head sadly.

"Oh, she isn't here, but do you know her? Linnea?"

The Breeze nodded happily and gave Sylvi a hug.

"She sent you to... comfort me?"

The Breeze nodded.

"Thank you. Please tell her I'm going to find the Troll. I just wish I could find Grandfather's journal," she added in an undertone.

The Breeze mimed looking for something.

"I would love some help looking, though I'm fairly certain it's a lost cause."

The Breeze gave her a haughty, insulted look that was so reminiscent of Linnea that it made Sylvi laugh.

"My apologies; I'm sure you can find it."

She wasn't sure of any such thing, but it felt good to say, and she smiled as she watched the Breeze rustle out to what was left of the ship and through the piles of provisions and wood scraps on the beach. When it disappeared into the woods, Sylvi assumed it had given up.

She threw one more rock into the water then turned to retrieve her pack.

A movement caught her eye just to the right of the place where the forest had made her cocoon. The Breeze was working hard to dislodge something from a lingonberry bush.

"My satchel!"

She ran the rest of the way, and only when she touched the bush did it relinquish its treasure.

Sylvi hugged it to herself.

"Thank you, noble guardian," she said to the bush, "for keeping this safe for me, and thank *you*, most observant of Breezes, for finding it. I thought for sure it was lost or damaged beyond repair."

She opened the bag and gently pulled out her grandfather's journal.

"It's perfect," she whispered, tears in her eyes.

The Breeze looked smug as it ruffled the bushes' leaves on its way to give Sylvi one last hug. It made a graceful leap into the air, caught a current and was off.

Sylvi waved until it was out of sight, then sat on the ground and started paging through the journal, looking for any notes about the Troll Castle.

"The Westerback forest has strong magical energies and is home to a wide array of mystical creatures."

As she read, the forest spirit's mushroom feelers made contact with Sylvi's bare feet.
It transmitted pictures of Nissa and Harpies, Rump Hobs and Gnomes.

"Are there wood Nymphs here? I'd love to meet them," she asked out loud while picturing her own dear companions from home- the birch maidens with their long limbs and the pine people, spikey hair sticking out in all directions.

Sylvi missed her sisters, but the Nymphs of the Fullanda woods had been her constant companions and protectors since she was in the cradle.
Missing them was like missing a part of herself.

The forest spirit sent a shady image of tree Nymphs swaying gently with their eyes closed.
Sylvi reached out with her senses, trying to feel if any were nearby.

"It's faint. Are they sleeping?"

The spirit didn't seem able to elaborate further. Sylvi decided to change tack. "It says here that the best way to reach the castle is to begin on the east side of the river, but it doesn't give any specific directions. Do you know the way?" She pictured the image she had received from the forest spirit of a princess serving a troll coffee in an enormous kitchen.

Gracefully, two aspens leaned their upper trunks towards each other, creating a leafy arch. Sylvi put the journal back in her satchel, collected her pack and headed through the living portal.

A trail of mushrooms appeared before her, leading into the forest. Sylvi smiled and began to follow.

Her bare feet tread softly on the path. Following the trail of mushrooms had been easy in the light, but as the sun went down, it got more difficult to find her way.

She looked around, searching for a good place to spend the night. As welcoming as the forest had been, Sylvi was quickly realizing how ill-prepared she was for adventuring in the wilderness. She loved nature and spent most of her days in the woods outside Fullanda Castle, but she had always been able to go inside to a warm meal and soft bed after dark.

Lost in thought, she didn't notice the pair of eyes in the gloom ahead until they were mere feet away. Soon, four more appeared a foot or so below the others.

It took a panic-stricken moment for her to realize that the eyes belonged to a beautiful roe deer doe with her twin fawns.

The mother walked up to Sylvi and paused a moment, staring at her with her liquid black eyes. She then turned and walked off, veering slightly to the left. The mushroom path seemed to agree with the deer's direction because it adjusted to follow her.

When Sylvi didn't start moving, the fawns nosed her hands, one on each side, pushing their soft heads under her palms. They walked forward so that her hands followed the curves of their red-brown dappled backs. They looked back at Sylvi as they followed their mother, entreating her to follow.

"Hello, where are you going?" she asked in the language known to the deer of Fullanda.

They either didn't understand her or weren't in the mood to talk. Deer were generally quiet creatures, and Sylvi couldn't sense anything sinister, so she decided to join them as they picked their way down an unseen path. It wasn't long before they came to a small clearing filled with a smorgasbord of late-bearing berry bushes.

Sylvi helped herself to bilberries, lingonberries and cloud berries, happily snacking next to the serene little family.

When they had all eaten their fill, the deer led her to a clear stream for a quick drink before bedding down for the night.

Once the sun had set, the air grew cold quickly. Sylvi took the blanket out of her pack and tried to get comfortable on the bed of bracken. The deer moved in close to share their warmth and companionship.

Sylvi spent two more nights with her new companions, but at last, they had strayed too far from their territory. The doe was anxious to return her children to the safety of known trails and sleeping grounds.

Waving goodbye, Sylvi sighed and then turned to continue following the trail of mushrooms. A large hare bounded onto the path ahead.

He waited until she drew up parallel to him, then turned and traveled alongside her down the trail.

Sylvi laughed. "It seems I'm not going to be trusted to travel alone. Thank you kindly for the escort."

The warmth of the hare that evening was not equal to that of the deer family, and Sylvi shivered under her thin blanket. Even in the cold, her exhaustion sent her quickly to sleep.

That morning she awoke with a start, sending a battalion of bunnies and hares into the underbrush. Only the original hare stayed snuggled up to her, leisurely stretching himself.

Sylvi chuckled all the way through her meager breakfast.

The days were getting colder and the forest thicker. Sylvi found herself falling into a pattern; wake up, mark the new day on her bracelet, eat a mouthful or two for breakfast, walk with an ever changing cast of animal companions until lunch and then eat what they could forage while walking until dark.

As her sack got lighter and foraging less fruitful, Sylvi started to worry that she might not make it to the troll castle after all.

At dusk one evening, while walking with a regal-looking lynx, she heard a strange sound drifting through the trees.

She stopped to listen more carefully, which disturbed the lynx. He tried to push on the backs of Sylvi's legs to get her moving down the path again.

"Do you hear that? It's, it's a violin. There must be a homestead or a cabin nearby."

Sylvi took two steps towards the music and stopped. The lynx had moved to block her way. Images of a faceless danger flashed into her head from the forest spirit.

"I know the mushrooms don't go in this direction, but I'm running out of supplies. I need to see if I can find where the music is coming from."

And, with that, Sylvi stepped around the wild cat, over the mushrooms and off the path.

15

Other People's Stories

Rania might have thought that she had imagined the fox speaking if a Breeze hadn't materialized next to her teacup and thrown it in a nearby bush.

"There you are!" she said to the Breeze. "I'm sorry if I scared you away. Is Linnea here?"

The Breeze shook its head.

"Does she need me? Is she in trouble?"

The Breeze shook its head and then started moving around wildly.

"I have no idea what that means," Rania said, biting her lip.

The fox cleared its throat. "I believe it's trying to say that someone, this Linnea perhaps, was attacked but then was able to throw the attackers... somewhere? That seems odd. Does that sound right?"

"Oh, you have no idea how right that sounds," Rania laughed.

The Breeze nodded enthusiastically.

"So, if she doesn't need me, why are you here?" Rania asked.

The Breeze flew over to Rania, hugged her and then turned to go.

"That's it?" Rania called after it.

The Breeze turned back and nodded.

"Alright, um, I guess, tell her I have a lead on finding the lindworm stone."

The Breeze nodded, mimed a giant angry dragon snake, and then flew off into the rapidly approaching night.

"That was odd," remarked the fox.

"You're a talking fox. You really think a pantomiming Breeze is odd?"

"Fair enough," he replied, a grin on his face.

"So, do *you* need my help? Are you under an enchantment that you need broken or something?" she asked him.

"Oh, no. I'm just here to help you get the seal skin back to the selkie."

"Oh, thank the stars, I *am* in the right place, but, wait, what makes you think I'm here to free a selkie?"

"You swam here from Selkie Island. A selkie gave you a necklace that transformed your skin color, and then you walked up to the homestead where an imprisoned selkie maiden is living. I certainly hope you're here to help her."

Rania shook her head, trying to break some understanding loose. It didn't work.

"So, you're going to help me?" she asked.

"I know where the seal skin is."

"Then what have you been waiting for???" she asked, throwing her hands in the air.

"Someone with hands who wouldn't be driven mad by a talking fox."

A slightly mad laugh burbled out of Rania. She found it hard to stop.

"Was I wrong?" the fox asked, looking concerned.

"Oh, no, you weren't wrong- I *do* have hands," Rania said, showing them to the fox and laughing harder.

The fox looked around, trying to see if he had missed something. When Rania didn't stop laughing, he asked, "Are you alright?"

Rania took a deep breath, held it and let out a long sigh.

"I'm just... I've always thought of myself as a heroine, but every day I seem to find myself a bit player in everyone else's story. I went from the Battle of the Air Princess and the North Wind to the Tale of the Selkie and the White Fox. I just found out that the air princess doesn't need my help, and the white fox only needs me for my hands. My own story doesn't even seem to belong to me. It's more about my mother; a princess who wanted children so badly she ate some rose buds from a cup. It worked, of course, but she later fell ill and now is in an enchanted sleep."

Rania sat down heavily on a rock. "I thought I could be the one to save her, but I keep getting side-tracked, so it will probably be some annoying prince who finds the cure, and my grandmother will be so grateful she'll give him my hand in marriage and half the kingdom, and I'll spend the rest of my days taking care of his seventeen children while he rides off to his next adventure."

"Your life sounds very complicated."

When it looked like Rania might start laughing again, he went on. "But that's a good thing. All the best stories are complicated. I don't know all the details of the stories you're living, but I'm glad they brought you here. The Selkie maid needs us. Now go get washed up before that old witch comes back. I'll find the tea cup and then keep watch."

16

Help from a Nameless Bird

The tournament grounds were packed, but Linnea was happy to find that Pahl wasn't wrong; a multitude of food stands dotted every path.

She stopped to buy skewered meatballs and a lingonberry pastry. After days on the road, the fresh, warm food was almost too much to take... almost. She had to remind herself that she was on a mission, or she might have stayed there sampling local delicacies all day.

As she rounded a corner, the crystal hill came into view.

"That thing is enormous!" she said aloud, then blushed in embarrassment.

Thankfully, everyone seemed too absorbed in their own business to notice her.

"Let's hope it stays that way." She mumbled under her breath.

Her plan depended on *not* being noticed. She wasn't sure how the people of this land felt about magic or people with elemental affinities, but Pahl's reaction to getting caught in the city after the festival started did not point to them being a forgiving people.

"Alright, Linnea, you can do this," she said to herself. "Step one, find a spot where I can see the contestants mount the hill." She looked around.

Panic crept in as every inch of ground in view of the action seemed occupied.

She wound through the crowd, searching for anywhere she might have a little privacy.

She found herself standing on an enormous half-moon shaped mound that almost looked like it was built up for the sole purpose of viewing the Crystal Hill. In the space between the mound and the hill stood an ornate structure filled with lavish seats under a canopy of gold brocade. The people occupying the seats looked like a living jewel box from this distance.

Linnea was happy to discover that the sight of them didn't cause envy or embarrassment for her current bedraggled state. The lavish fabrics and ornamentation seemed ridiculous for a day this warm.

At the very center of the platform sat a man who could only be the king. His seat was taller than the rest, and he wore a heavy crown on his head. Even at this distance, Linnea didn't much like the look of him. She was trying to decide why when a flamboyantly dressed announcer called out in a carrying voice.

"Official word is in from the hill. Sir Gumay maintains his lead by a hair's breadth. Will our next contender be the one to pass him?"

Loud cheers erupted from the crowd.

Linnea put out a prayer to any powers that were listening that the next contender wasn't Pahl.

"Undaunted by near-fatal bad luck in previous years, for his first attempt of the day, I give you... Sir Sven of the Tove Valley!"

A lukewarm cheer followed the announcement, along with some ill-disguised snickering.

Linnea sensed that the crowd was anxious to see him fail. She rolled her eyes and redoubled her efforts to find a good spot.

"It seems," the announcer went on, "that he has outfitted his horse with textured hoof enhancements."

"Is that allowed?" a spectator with a big hat asked her neighbor. "Seems like cheating to me."

"It won't do him any good," was the response. "Just you watch."

A fanfare was blown on long trumpets, and the announcer picked up his commentary. "The noble knight is off. His stallion races towards the hill, tail streaming behind him. They are reaching the base and are leaping up the incline. One, two, three strides. Oh, no, they have stumbled and are rolling back down the hill! Healers are running in to attend both horse and rider."

"What did I say," boasted the spectator's friend. "The fancier the get-up, the more entertaining the fall!"

"You are horrid," laughed her friend. "That poor man! Do you think he's alright?"

"Probably not," she replied heartlessly. "I don't know why he enters every year. It always ends the same way. You should have been here last year."

Linnea had no interest in hearing about last year, so she jostled through the crowd, now desperate for a secluded spot.

"Everyone on your feet, and give your best Gyldenfare cheer because Prince Karl Erik of Osterlanda has entered the grounds!"

If Linnea had thought the crowd was loud before, it was nothing to the monumental din that rose from this announcement. She put her hands over her ears to try muffling it. When it died down a bit, she felt something land on her head. She had already batted at it before realizing it was the blue bird.

"Where have you been?" Linnea scolded. "I was worried about you."

The bird paid her no attention as it flew to a high outcropping of rock near the back of the crowd.

Linnea followed and soon realized there was a small indent halfway up that had a perfect view of the hill while being shielded from most festivalgoers.

She wondered why no one had grabbed the spot before realizing it would be an almost impossible climb.

"Guess it's time to find some Breezes."

17

A Red Water Lilly

The sound of the violin filled Sylvi with longing. She struggled on through the forest, eagerly trying to find the source. As the sun began to rise, she saw a flash of water in a clearing ahead. A quick stop for a drink, and then she would be back on her way. She *must* find where the music was coming from.

As she stumbled into the clearing, dirty and disheveled, a glorious sight met her tired eyes; sitting in a small lake, surrounded by red-flowered water lilies, was a man, completely absorbed in the music he was playing on his violin.

His body swayed as the bow slid across his instrument, back and forth.

Sylvi stopped, transfixed, and sank to her knees. The music surrounded and filled her. She wanted it to go on forever.

She stared at the man, only now noticing that his chest was bare. The lower portion of his body was beneath the water, and Sylvi realized, with a blush, that it was probably bare as well.

His hair was long and straight, falling to one side of his face like a mane. She leaned forward to see him better and fell headlong into the pool.

The music stopped abruptly as Sylvi spluttered, righting herself.

"Oh, *please*, don't stop." She begged.

The man smiled. "Who are you, little one, who has wandered so far from salvation?"

Sylvi looked up to find he was quite close, offering her a hand to assist her to her feet. His eyes were dazzling, like the pool he stood in.

"P...pardon?" she stammered. She hadn't quite heard what he said.

"Few who find my lake ever want to leave. What is your name, little one?"

What was it she always told her sisters about names? She couldn't quite remember.

"I might ask you the same," she replied.

"Ah, but I would not answer you, for to hear my name uttered by mortal lips would mean my end. Are you mortal? Do mortals come in green? I've been alone so long, I really can't recall. You have such lovely lips, pretty thing; perhaps my devastation would almost be worth it, coming from them."

Sylvi didn't like the idea of bringing him devastation.

"Come closer, my pet. You are a pretty little thing, if a bit peculiar."

"I beg your pardon." Linnea always called her peculiar with a wrinkled nose. Linnea?

Sylvi shook her head, trying to clear the cobwebs.

"Oh, don't worry, I think it quite adorable. Come here, child. Let me see those lips of yours."

Something made her pause. She didn't want to get closer to him. Perhaps it was just easier to gaze at him from a few steps away.

"Um, no, thank you. I'm looking for something."
Was she looking for something? Strange, she
couldn't remember. Why did she say that?

"And you've found me. Good job. Now you can
come here, and I can reward you."

"No," she said, still not knowing why. "I've got
important... must be... need to find." She swayed a
bit on her feet. She really had been walking a long
time.

"Oh, you poor thing. Here, take a sip of water
from my pool. It's just what you need."

He scooped water into his hand and held it out
to her. She took a step forward, reaching to bring
his hand up to her lips, and that's when she saw it
- the plain, sodden leather band around her wrist.
The rough hash marks brought back the image of
showing her sisters how they could mark their
bracelets to keep track of the days.

"My mother!" she yelled, drawing back and
turning to go. "I need to leave."

She made it halfway to the trees before the
music began again.

She stopped and turned.

"Did I not say that there is no salvation here?"

A slow smile worked its way across the face of
the man in the water. Like the smile, his words
were languorous, as if they had nowhere to go.

"I have had sorceresses and queens; a child like
you is hardly a distraction for me, but if I decide I
desire you to stay, then you have little choice in the
matter. This is where it ends for you, my little one."

Sylvi sank to the ground, not wanting her legs
to betray her and bring her back to the lake. She
grasped her bracelet as a talisman, and her head

began to clear. When she looked at the man now, all she saw was loneliness.

"I'm guessing you *could* force me to stay, but I'd like to believe that you won't. I don't think you really enjoy playing the part of the sinister, enchanting villain. You seem much more suited to the role of...," here she pursed her lips for a moment, "of the mysterious stranger who gives a weary traveler a glimpse into his intriguingly exotic world and then respects her need to be on her way."

When the man said nothing and merely blinked at Sylvi, she gave him a smile and a shrug.

The man's face split into a surprised and delighted grin. He laughed as he said, "Who or what are you, little one?"

"I am no one," Sylvi answered.

"You speak false, child. You are *radiant!*"

Now it was Sylvi's turn to laugh. "Me? What about you? *You* are amazing! Your music transports the soul, and I know it's forward of me, but, may I just say that you don't need power or guile to find companionship. It will find you. I can feel it in my heart."

The man paused for a moment, then said, "Stop. I release you. Go find your... mother, was it?"

"Not find her, but cure her. She lays in an enchanted sleep, but we don't have much time. I'm on my way to Saumlina Castle to convince a troll to sell me a magic stone."

The man smiled conspiratorially and picked one of the red water lilies from the pool.

"Here. Take this. Waft its scent toward any living creature, and it will fall instantly to sleep for one hour. I hope you will not need it, or, if you do, that an hour is enough."

Sylvi took the flower, a radiant smile on her face. "Thank you!"

"I wish you all the luck that is mine to give. Go make this mother of yours well again, little one, for if she has half the spirit of her daughter, this world has sore need of her."

Sylvi, unaccustomed to compliments, simply said, "I wish I had something I could give you."

The man thought for a while, a smirk flitting across his face before his honest and natural smile returned. "Your name, perhaps?"

She didn't hesitate to reply, "Sylvi. My name is Sylvi."

"Then fare you well, bright Sylvi. I see someone is looking for you."

He gestured to the side of the lake where a trail of mushrooms had appeared.

Sylvi started to walk towards it, then stopped and turned back to the man.

"I'm afraid it will be a long time, if ever, before I hear your music again. Would you mind... could you play me one last song?"

Sylvi wasn't sure, but she thought she saw a small flush of red color the man's cheeks.

"I'll do you better than that. I will play you a hero's tune to get you back on your way."

And this time, when the music filled her ears, it did not fill her with longing but with the feeling that she was uniquely fit for the task ahead.

18

Avoiding Forgetfulness

"Was it poisoned- the tea?" Rania asked the fox as she slipped into the warm water. It felt heavenly on her aching muscles.

"Not precisely," the fox mumbled from the bushes. "It's a draft of forgetfulness. I'm guessing she was hoping to have two unpaid servants and a brand-new pearl necklace. Ah, here's the teacup."

He came trotting back to the hot spring, earthenware mug dangling from his mouth. He gently placed it in the spot it had been, averting his eyes from the bathing girl.

Rania splashed about merrily, scrubbing up and rinsing off.

"Ha!" she yelled out when she started combing her hair. "I forgot about you!" With a bit of pulling and cursing, she produced a small pouch that she had tied into her braid. She opened it and poured the glistening contents into her hand. "Take that, Linnea!"

When the fox snorted, Rania explained. "My sister thought I was crazy wanting to hide away some of the treasure our grandfather gave us."

"Keep that well hidden," said the fox, "or she won't bother with a forgetting potion; you'll get the same fate as my dear departed Mistress M."

"I'm guessing she didn't get to live out her days with sunshine, puppies and a happily ever after," Rania said, slipping the gems back into the pouch.

"She did live long, and most of it was happy, but no one really gets *ever* after. Just the same, being pushed from a cliff is not what most people envision as a happy ending. Unless you have some more of those Breeze fellows about. I'd love to see the look on her face if she pushed you off and you just flew away."

"Nah, the Breezes never listen to me, just my sister Linnea. They're more likely to help her throw me off a cliff than help me fly. Nixies are my pals, you know, water spirits. I wonder if there are any here."

Rania reached out with her mind, and two plump Nixies floated up from the bottom of the spring, eyes at half mast, with large grins on their faces.

"Hot Spring Nixies! Good to meet you. I'm Rania."

They nodded at her slowly and disappeared back under the water.

"Wait," said the fox, "I thought you told the old hag that your name was Sylvi."

"Oh, right. That's my other sister- the nice one. She says that it's dangerous to give out your true name and impolite to ask for another's."

"She's very smart. Most people don't know what to do with a name, but others...." He shivered at the thought. "Since I now know your name, I will tell you mine; it's Kai. Well, I'm not exactly sure what my original name was, but Mistress M always called me Kai. Oh, and be sure to collect all of that hair. Don't leave even a strand on the comb when you give it back."

"So, she's an enchantress?" Rania asked.

"Nothing so lofty or powerful; she's a common earth witch, but she's twisted her magics into something bitter and evil."

They heard a door slam in the distance.

"Quick, gather up the loose hair and give it to me. I'll bury it deep. Tomorrow is market day in the small town across the island. The witch will be away all day. Ensure you stay behind so I can show you where the seal skin is." And with that, he was gone.

Rania finished rinsing her hair and was putting on the dressing gown when Ebba arrived, carrying a lantern.

"You were gone so long I thought you may 'a drowned." She laughed a cold chuckle and went on, "Brought a lantern to light our way back. Good, good, I see you drank up your tea."

Rania had no idea how strong the tea was. Was the effect gradual, or should she be forgetting what a foot was called after one cup?

She decided to play it safe.

"I am so sorry; I accidentally spilled it when getting into the water. I feel horrible, but at least the cup didn't chip."

Rania couldn't see Ebba's face since she walked in front of her with the lantern, but the woman didn't falter in her step. Was Kai right about the tea?

The cabin looked cozy, with its windows gleaming orange in the darkening night.

The smell of the soup was intoxicating as they entered the kitchen. There was a brief moment before the spoon hit her mouth when Rania wondered if the soup was also tainted with forgetting potion, but she chose to believe it safe as she shoveled down several helpings.

She also worried about the woman killing her in her sleep for about a second before her head hit the pillow.

A storm raged in the night, but Rania slept like a woman who had been hit on the head, dragged through the ocean by Nixies, and finally had a hot bath, a good meal and a soft bed.

The cock crowing outside the window woke her with a start. It took her a moment to remember where she was.

She followed the sounds of pans clanking against each other and found the Selkie and Ebba cleaning up after a sparse breakfast.

"We are away this morning," Ebba informed her. "Tis market day, and we can'afford to miss it. You drink up your tea now, and we'll be off."

The mug of steaming beverage sat on the table in a beam of light.

"It's brewed extra strong since you missed the healin' dose last night. Drink it up!"

Ebba stared at Rania, suspicion in every line of her bony face. It was clear she wasn't going to leave until Rania drank the tea.

Knowing full well that Kai had been right about the draught, Rania took a small sip.

"Yum," she said.

Ebba wasn't taking any chances. "Drink it all down now. It's got healing herbs. We want you to get better right quick."

Rania went through the options in her head as she lifted the cup for another sip. None of them were good, and all except drinking the tea would blow her cover. She needed them to leave so she and Kai could retrieve the seal skin.

She downed the liquid in one big gulp and put the mug on the table.

A wave of dizziness went through her, and she tottered a bit.

"We better get you back to bed while the medicine does its work," said Ebba, guiding Rania back to the sleeping cot.

Rania crawled under the covers gratefully, eyes shut tight against the spinning.

"Should we leave her alone?" the Selkie asked. "She doesn't look well. I could stay with her."

"She'll be fine, and I need you to help carry our provisions back from the market. There won't be another one for a month, so we need to stock up. You just rest now, dearie, we'll be home before night fall."

Rania could hear the click of the door shutting. She knew what she had to do, but she didn't like it. Rolling over, she forced herself to vomit into the ash pan. The results were immediate. The dizziness subsided, but she made herself stumble outside and vomit again in the bushes.

When Kai trotted up she was sitting on the stoop, sipping water.

"I smell something foul. Are you alright?" he asked.

"I don't know. Ebba made me drink the tea. I threw it up again, but I had to wait a while. How do I know if it's working?"

"It usually puts the drinker into a deep sleep, and when they awake, their memories have faded."

"I wanted to go to sleep; I was so dizzy."

"But you didn't?"

"I didn't."

"And you seem to remember me," the fox commented. "If we keep you awake you should be fine just as long as you don't get another dose."

Rania sighed. "Let's get that sealskin and get away from this island so it never comes to that."

"I wish I could swim away like a selkie," said Kai.

"You can't swim?"

"I can swim, just not far enough. I came to this island in a year, where the sea in this region froze over completely. I wasn't from this area, so I thought it happened every year. I was wrong. I've been stuck here ever since."

"That's horrible- stuck on an island with a woman who throws stones at you and calls you vermin."

"That's just a recent development. I came when Mistress M lived in the cottage. She was wonderful. We had many fine years together. This witch, she was the mistress's apprentice, and she was alright to begin with, but this island holds old magics, and some are corrupted by it. Come, I'll show you the sealskin. It might make a bit more sense once you see the place. Do you feel well enough? It's a bit of a climb."

As they walked, Kai told Rania of how his human parents had angered an earth witch, and instead of doing something to *them*, she cursed their firstborn.

"Which is completely unfair, if you ask me. Why involve an innocent unborn child? At any rate, at the age of thirteen, the curse came into effect, and I was transformed into a fox."

Kai paused to let Rania catch up before continuing. "I was angry, so I set out to find the witch who had cursed me and make her turn me back. I tracked her to this island, and, as fate would have it that very winter was the one I told you about, so I walked over and found the witch's cottage. She lay dying, attended by her apprentice, Mistress M."

"Did she refuse to change you back?" Rania asked.

"No, she saw my point and told me what I needed to do to break the spell before she died. Strangely, I found myself reluctant to change back. I thought that maybe I would just finish out the winter as a fox since my coat was so warm. Soon, years had gone by, and I realized I liked being a fox, and I liked my life on the island, even if there aren't any lemmings here."

Rania laughed. "You miss lemmings?"

"Don't mock it until you've tried it. Lemmings are the finest dining the northern world has to offer."

"You *eat* them? But they're adorable," Rania protested.

"Adorably delicious," Kai said as he trotted off ahead of her.

They climbed a steep outcropping and had to stop to catch their breath.

"It's just around the next bend," Kai said.

When they got to a smooth rock ledge, Kai stood on his back paws to nose at a crack in the rock.

"You must put your hand in there," he instructed.

When she did, her fingers caught on a small latch. She had to prod it in several directions before it gave a click, and a seam appeared in the rock.

"Are you sure this is safe?" Rania asked.

"No," Kai replied, "but this is where she hid the seal skin."

Rania gritted her teeth and pulled open the door. It was filled, floor to ceiling, with seal skins.

Rania's stomach lurched.

Looking at the multitude of pelts kindled a horror deep within. She wanted to shut the door and run as far away as possible.

"How can we even tell which one belongs to our selkie maiden?" asked Kai with a note of sadness in his voice.

Rania swallowed her revulsion and forced herself to really look at the skins. Most of them were old, dusty and moth-eaten, but one shone with a glossy glow.

"That one," Rania said, reaching for it.

"Wait! There could be a trap," Kai warned. They both studied the cave for anything out of the ordinary.

Finally, Rania said, "I have no idea what a spell or trap might look like. I'm just going to grab it."

Kai rolled a shoulder. Even in their short relationship the gesture had become familiar to Rania. She thought of it as his fox shrug.

"Alright, but be careful," he said.

Rania delicately reached for the skin. As she pulled it back through the entrance it glowed for a moment, startling them both. When nothing else happened, Rania closed the door, and they began their climb back down in silence.

It felt safer to talk when they made it to the hot springs.

"What do you think that glow was?" Rania asked the fox.

Kai just shook his head.

"All those skins...," Rania began, but just let the thought trail off.

"They must have been there for years," Kai said tentatively, "far longer than *this* witch has been on the island. Since she was Mistress M's apprentice, it makes me wonder...," Kai paused, looking for words. "Mistress M was my friend. It hurts to think that she might have been part of something so sinister."

Rania wasn't sure what to do. She knew that she should comfort Kai, reassure him, or say *something*, but she was never good in these types of situations. She didn't know if his friend had a dark past or not. Every comforting word she thought of felt dishonest.

Rania took a breath and tried her best.

"We don't know how those skins got there. It could have been a crypt for departed selkies, or maybe it *was* something sinister. I think the important thing is to get this live skin back to its owner so she can be free. Once I've saved my mother, I'll come back, and we can figure it out together."

Kai nodded gravely. "And you've got my help in your quest, if you want it."

"It's a deal," she said, smiling. "Well, what do we do now, my clever fox?"

Kai blinked. "I hadn't really thought of that."

They walked on in silence until the house came into view.

"You know," said Kai, "I felt a pull of magic when the skin left the cave. I'm guessing that the witch knows something is amiss and will cut their market trip short."

"That might not be a bad thing unless you think she'll hurt the selkie," said Rania.

"Only if cornered," Kai mused. "She seems to enjoy having someone to order around. We should be more worried about her trying to hurt one of us."

Rania walked behind the house to get a better look at the path down to the ocean.

"Alright," she said. "We need to get the selkie to the water so she can put on her seal skin and escape."

"That might be difficult if the old crone is on to you. Her magic isn't strong, but she's not afraid to play dirty."

Rania smiled, "If we can get them to the water, we'll have reinforcements."

"Could we use her greed against her?" Kai asked. "What happened to those baubles you found while bathing?"

Rania bristled. She didn't know what kind of supplies she might need for her journey north.

"That's all the money I have," she told him.

"You wouldn't have to use *all* of it."

Rania sighed and nodded her head. "What do you have in mind?"

19

The Scholar & His Steed

There were dozens of Breezes, all vying to help Linnea with her plan. They were so enthusiastic that it was hard to keep them all focused.

The first step had been easy. All she needed them to do was help her scale the rocky outcropping. The next bit, however, involved some serious coordination. As the announcer took to the stage again, Linnea motioned to the Breezes to get a move on.

"Ladies and Gentle Folk, it has come to our attention that a late contender has entered the lists. It is our *honor* to announce Gyldenfare's very own mapmaker and scholar- Pahl Christiansson!"

A murmur bubbled up from the crowd. The only words Linnea could make out were, "Is he serious???" and "He's not wearing any armor."

The announcer, pleased with the effect his words had on the crowd, now tried his best to ramp up their enthusiasm.

"After a bow to the royal box, they are off! The Scholar and his steed gallop full tilt towards the treacherous hill!"

Linnea drew in a breath and started orchestrating Breezes to help Pahl and Bert along their way. She tried to block out the announcer's fevered commentary, but it was hard to ignore.

"They have made it to the base of the hill! One, two, three gallops up!"

As the horse gained height Linnea thought the Breezes might lose control, but they held tight and kept the unsteady duo moving.

"Five, six, they're past the high mark! Ten, eleven, twelve! No one has ever made it this high in the festival's history, folks!"

In the excitement, the whole crowd began counting with the announcer.

"Fifteen, sixteen- they just might make it all the way! Nineteen, twenty, twenty one, twenty two, twenty Three!!!!! They are at the top!!! The courageous mapmaker plucks a golden apple from the tree. He is holding it up so all can see."

The crowd had been shocked into silence, but at the sight of the apple in the mapmaker's hand, they went wild.

Linnea let out her breath, a relieved smile starting to form on her face until the announcer's words reminded her with a jolt that her job wasn't complete.

"Quiet, Folks! It is time for the descent. This is possibly the most dangerous moment of the day."

Linnea quickly motioned for the celebrating Breezes to help the horse and rider back down the hill. Not all of them saw her in time, but enough were paying attention to get Pahl and Bert down safely.

Both horse and rider seemed shocked and a bit unsteady as Pahl dismounted and presented the apple to the king.

Linnea couldn't quite tell, but she thought she saw the king nod his head to the unlikely champion as he took the golden apple from him.

The rowdy crowd quieted as the king rose from his seat and addressed them.

"Did we ever think this day would come? A champion of champions in the guise of a humble mapmaker."

The king then took his daughter's hand and presented it to Pahl.

He kissed it and then let it go.

"To be of service to my king," he said in a carrying voice, "is the only reward I desire and to have Princess Astrid marry or not, as she chooses."

The crowd was confused by his words, and it took a while to quiet them enough to hear Astrid's response.

"It would be an honor to marry such a fine champion."

Even from a distance, Linnea could see that the princess was beaming with happiness.

"Father, at your will, please name the day."

The crowd cheered as the princess took Pahl's hand and held it high. Linnea saw him whisper something in her ear before the royal box was obscured by wandering festival-goers.

It was a bit trickier for Linnea to get down from her lofty perch than it had been to climb up, but she managed it without looking too conspicuous, or that's what she thought until a royal guard approached her.

"Is your name Linnea?" he asked.

She instantly regretted not asking Pahl about the town's feelings on people who use magic and elemental powers.

She turned and gave him a bright smile. "What is this about, my fine sir?" she asked.

"I've been sent to retrieve you," was all he said.

"Who has sent for me? And where are you retrieving me to?" she asked, looking for an exit route through the teeming crowd.

"I've been sent to retrieve you," he repeated. "Come with me."

"Alright, I guess I will be retrieved, then. Lead the way."

The guard clearly thought she was a flight risk as he made her walk ahead of him. The crowd parted as they saw the guard, leaving them an easy path. Linnea's dread grew.

The terrain was filled with rolling hills, and as they crested one of them, a sea of marvelous tents lay before them like a patchwork city.

At the center of the colorful array was a pavilion and open-air dancing platform hung with lanterns.

"It must be stunning at night when they're all lit," Linnea said aloud.

The guard didn't even grunt in acknowledgment, but he did point toward the largest tent to let her know which way to go.

As they got closer, Linnea realized it wasn't the large tent they were headed for but a smaller one in the same color of brilliant crimson.

There was, in fact, a long line of crimson tents, each with a guard standing at attention out front. As they approached the last and smallest in the row, its guard clicked his heels together and asked, "Name?"

His manner automatically triggered her into giving her official title.

"The Princess Linnea Gunvor Margareta of Fullanda."

She screamed at herself internally, but now that it was out, she would have to commit. She straightened her spine, wondering if the guard would balk at this ragged girl claiming to be a princess.

He didn't even raise an eyebrow as he opened the tent flap and announced, "The Princess Linnea Gunvor Margareta of Fullanda to see the Princess Royal of Gyldenfare, Astrid Margrethe Isabelle Elizabeta."

A refined voice issued from inside the tent. "She may enter."

The tent guard opened the flap wide. It was darker inside, taking Linnea a moment for her eyes to adjust.

While she was still getting her bearings, a whirlwind of a girl rushed up and grabbed her hands.

"Pahl'ley didn't tell me you were a princess and one of the missing princesses, no less! How remarkable! I was so worried when I heard that you and your sisters had disappeared, but how could I have known that the universe itself was sending you to deliver me from my miserable fate?!?"

The girl didn't even draw breath as she dragged Linnea to a padded folding stool and made her sit. "Loaning your magical horse to Pahl'ley was a pure act of charity! I can never repay you for your kindness! Never! Oh, how rude of me. Would you like to freshen up or have a sip of wine?"

Linnea blinked, still trying to process it all. It amused her to think of Bert as magical, but she was happy to let the misunderstanding stand. Slowly, she said, "That would be lovely, but I'm afraid that no amount of freshening is going to help this dress. I was in a shipwreck and have traveled far since then without the aid of 'freshening' facilities."

Astrid's face lit up. "Well, there is a warm copper tub all filled with scented water waiting behind that screen."

Linnea almost swooned, but before she could answer, the tent guard made another announcement.

"His High Royal Majesty, the King Fritjof of Gyldenfare, to see his youngest royal daughter and her most distinguished guest."

Astrid's face went white, but she answered, "One moment," and shoved Linnea behind the bathing screen.

"I should have known the guard would squeal. If I say you are indisposed, he can't press to see you, then we can get you out tonight while everyone else is at the ball."

Without another word, she ran to the tent flap, and with a flash of light from outside, she was gone.

Though it was a very fine tent, it was still only made of fabric. From behind the bathing screen, Linnea could hear everything.

"Father, how lovely to see you. Can I be of assistance?"

The king's voice was rough and curt. "I hear that you have a most distinguished young lady visiting you. I have come to invite her, personally, to the evening's festivities."

"What a lovely and gracious gesture, your highness," she replied. "Thank you for thinking of her. However, she is much wearied from her travels and, I fear, in no condition to attend such a glorious affair."

"Nonsense. She *will* attend. I will see you both at the dining pavilion in one hour. I know how much you ladies love dancing and finery. I am sure that the Princess Linnea would not want to miss a moment of the festivities. Do not deny her this, Astrid. It is most unbecoming."

Before Astrid could reply, Linnea heard the king's retinue shuffle back into movement and march away.

Astrid stormed back into the tent and whispered, "Nothing stays secret in this place! We'll have to get you out tonight *after* the ball. I hate to cut your bathing time short, but we'll need to get you cleaned up quickly if we're going to be on time. You jump in the tub and I'll go raid my sisters' tents for a gown and a maid to do your hair. I hope Inga is free- she's the best and the fastest. I'll be back in no time. You have a quick soak."

As Astrid left the tent, a small shadow flew in and perched on the changing screen. Linnea was happy to see the familiar face.

"How did you get in without being announced?" she teased. "I'm disappointed; then I would have known your true name."

The bird preened, ignoring her entirely.

"Fine, pretend you don't care, but I'll always remember that it was you who found that amazing out-cropping at the festival. I never could have helped Pahl win without your help."

The bird continued minding its own business, so Linnea started peeling off her dust-caked shoes and stockings. The smell was almost too much to bear. How long had she been in these clothes???

Because her escapades with Rania generally called for disguises, she was an expert at removing even the most torturous garments without assistance. Her aching muscles protested at the process, but a bit of struggle and some words unbecoming a princess later, her filthy dress lay on the floor.

The water felt sublime. Linnea knew she had to make it quick, but her body demanded that she take a few moments to simply relax.

Astrid came back, in what seemed like no time, with her arms full of beautiful things. She dropped them unceremoniously on the floor.

"Inga will be here as soon as she is done with my sisters."

"How many sisters do you have?" Linnea asked, trying to scrub her fingernails clean.

"Eleven," was the reply. "Half-sisters, really; my father has been married *many* times and is now, again, a widower. He is determined to get his bloodline into as many royal families as possible, which is why he was so angry when Pahl won the tournament. If Sir Gummay had won, it would have expanded his reach to the west."

"So, is he angry at me for helping Pahl?" Linnea asked.

"Oh, no, he doesn't know about the enchanted horse you loaned him. Well, I assume it was the horse. Was it actually a magic saddle or reins?"

Linnea smiled, relieved that they didn't guess the truth. When she didn't answer right away, Astrid went on.

"Fullanda has always been a problem for my father because your grandmother made it abundantly clear that your mother was not 'for sale.' Now he finds *you* on his doorstep, of marrying age and seemingly friendless. He will not let you go easily."

Linnea's muscles started to tense back up. "What can I do?"

"Play along for now, and remember that you are *not* friendless. Pahley and I will figure this out."

20

A Princess Named Boots

Sylvi dreamed of being warm and comfortable in her bed at the castle. She smiled and rolled over, cozying into the soft blankets. When her bedding started moving, Sylvi awoke with a start, hitting her head on a branch. She seemed to be surrounded by branches.

Slowly, they started to open up, changing her cocoon into more of a nest. It all started coming back to her. She had found it this way last night at the end of a long walk, a nest of bushes lined with the downy feathers of every manner of bird. It must have closed around her as she slept.

As the cold morning air hit her face, Sylvi almost asked the branches to stop opening.

She stretched, and when her bare toes peaked out of her woolen blanket, she rapidly pulled them back in again.

One toe slowly poked out, testing the air, and Sylvi sighed. She knew this day would come, but she had hoped to put it off a bit longer.

Digging in her pack, she pulled out a pair of thick socks and some soft leather boots. She knew she would be grateful for their warmth, but she would miss having that direct connection with the earth.

Before leaving her nest, she took out her sharp rock and marked the day on her bracelet. She gently smoothed her thumb over the marks and thought of her sisters.

Rolling up her blanket, she marveled at how easily it fit in the pack these days. She dug out some dried fish and her last small hunk of bread, and then washed it down with the last sips of water from her skin.

When the mushroom guides showed her a path, she asked, "Could you bring me by a stream or river?"

They disappeared all at once, and then popped up in a line that veered more to the right.

Sylvi thanked her nest, which looked more like a collection of bushes every moment, and dutifully followed her fungal friends. She now knew why this forest had a reputation for being haunted. Every living thing here was bursting with spirit.

It wasn't long before the tinkling of running water reached her ears. As she bent to refill her water supply, a loud creaking noise startled her. It wasn't a forest sound. She quickly closed her water skin and scrambled up the small hill on the other side of the stream.

Yellow leaves gently rained down upon her, joining their siblings on the golden carpeted ground. She stumbled on the way up, but made it to the top without much of a fuss.

The trees were thinner up there, and she could easily see a stone castle in a clearing not far off. It was surrounded by a moat, and the creaking she heard was the sound of an enormous drawbridge being lowered.

Sylvi's skin shifted to the colors of her surroundings. It occurred to her that she hadn't used her camouflage since the day her grandfather returned with his dire news. Before then, she had been using it nearly every day to avoid her sisters' antics. She wondered now what she had missed.

Sylvi crept forward for a better look. The drawbridge was fully lowered.

She had never seen a troll, but she had read about them extensively. She was happy that this one, though quite large, was not of the giant variety and that he only had one head.

Halfway across the bridge, the troll stopped and gave an enormous sneeze. Before the echo of the first had died, three more erupted in rapid succession. As Sylvi watched, a small figure dressed all in delicate pinks ran out to the troll and handed him a bath towel sized handkerchief. She seemed to scold him, presumably for leaving without it, then ran back to the heavy wooden doors and shut herself inside.

Sylvi wondered at the girl's haste until the earsplitting trumpeting of the troll blowing his nose nearly knocked her off her feet.

She put her fingers in her ears, bracing for more, but the troll merely put the cloth in his pocket, picked up a large basket, and marched off into the wood.

Waiting until she could no longer hear the Troll crashing through the forest (punctuated by sneezes), Sylvi crept towards the castle.

She felt exposed as she crossed the drawbridge, even with her skin in camouflage mode. When she got to the enormous double doors, she was sorely tempted to run away. Fortunately, she noticed a smaller door off to the right, which looked decidedly less intimidating. She walked up to it, willed her skin to a healthy shade of peach, and knocked confidently while calling out, "Hello, is anyone there?"

Her heart raced as she waited, but no one answered. She tried again, this time louder- still nothing. After a few more tries she kicked the door in frustration, which led to many minutes of hopping and nursing a hurt toe.

With a whispered expletive and a frustrated hrumph, she slumped onto the ground with her back against the door. Quite suddenly, it opened from within, spilling her onto her back.

She looked up to see the pink-clad person with a laundry basket on their hip staring down at her.

Up close the person could never be mistaken for a girl. His sandy hair was long, but the slight shadow of facial hair emphasized his jawline, and his voice was decidedly masculine.

"Well, hello there. I thought I heard something out here. Sorry to give you a spill. Can I help you up?"

He didn't wait for her to answer but reached down, offering his hand.

Sylvi was still trying to process what she saw when the boy (for he wasn't *quite* a man yet) flashed her a smile that rendered thought difficult. She gave him her hand, and he helped her to her feet.

"May I just ask," he said, looking her up and down, "do you always dress as a boy? I mean, not to be rude, I'm just curious. Obviously," he continued, gesturing to his dress, "I'm not averse to experimental attire, but *my* clothing choices come with an exciting story. I'm just wondering if yours do, too."

"So... you're not an average, everyday princess doing laundry for her troll?" Sylvi asked.

"You have a discerning eye, I see. No, there is nothing average or everyday about me, and," here he looked around as if spying out eavesdroppers then leaned in to whisper, "I am not really a princess. Thank the gods; horrible things, princesses, worse than trolls."

Sylvi's face must have hinted at the offense she was feeling because the boy rushed on.

"Terribly sorry, miss, we haven't been formally introduced. Maybe I should go back inside, and we can try again, shall we?"

The boy must have interpreted Sylvi's blink as a 'yes' because he grabbed his laundry basket and flashed her one more dazzling grin before shutting the door in her face.

"Oh, no, so sorry!" came his muffled voice from behind the door. "That was more forceful than intended. I'm not used to guests."

Sylvi wasn't sure how to proceed. She was about to knock when the door opened again, and the boy stuck his head out.

"We're taking it from the part where you knock. OK, go." He shut the door again with exaggerated care.

With a smile, Sylvi raised her hand and gave the door a few short raps.

When it opened this time, the boy had assumed an exaggeratedly formal manner.

"Well, hello, fine lady or sir. To what do we owe the honor of your visit?"

Sylvi let a small smile slip but then fell comfortably into the play-acting.

"I am here on business, good sir or madam, or is it *Majesty*?"

"High Exalted One will do," he quipped.

"Very well, oh High Exalted One. Is the Troll of the household at leisure to see me?"

"Alas," he replied in mock sadness, "he is out for the day, as he is every day. Perhaps this business of yours is something I can help you with, or, at the very least, may I offer you some refreshments while you wait?"

"Thank you kindly,' she replied. "That would be most appreciated."

The boy offered her his arm.

"In all seriousness, my name is Boots, Storyteller First Class."

"And I am pri... Ellinsdotter, Sylvi. You can just call me Sylvi."

21

Baubles as Bait

Rania sat on a rock looking out at the sea. She longed to jump into the cold waves and swim away from it all.

When did the world get so dark? She'd known the story of the healing crown since childhood, but it always seemed like a story about a woman whose love for her husband and kingdom gave her the strength to do the impossible. She'd never really given any thought to the end of the story; the part where the princes, Rania's own great, great uncles, let greed get in the way of returning the stones that had been loaned to them in good faith- the stones that kept other kingdoms safe and prosperous.

Rania stroked the sealskin she held in her arms. She'd always had a profound respect for witches and other magic users, but the thought of that cave and the hundreds of dead skins made her stomach turn. Were they all enslaved, or was it something even worse?

At least the whole ordeal was almost over, and then she could get back on track- find the Lindworm, get the stone, bring it to Fullanda, save her mother, return the stone to its rightful kingdom.

She looked at her hands. She had almost gotten used to them looking so creamy tan. She played with the pearl necklace that kept her that color.

Why had she never really thought about how different she and her sisters were?

The sound of pebbles clicking together drew her out of her reverie.

"I have to give you credit." Ebba's voice had changed from rustic to refined, and so had her bearing. She looked powerfully angry, and she had a knife.

"You really had me convinced you were a castaway, but did you think I'd be stupid enough to bring the girl with me into this 'trap' of yours?"

Rania's shoulders slumped fractionally, but no words came to her.

"Thank you for the trinkets," Ebba went on, shuffling the gems in her hand, "but what I really want is my sealskin back. So, if you would be so kind... Give it to me NOW!"

Rania could feel the words of power in the witch's command, but she made no move to relinquish the pelt she had clutched in her arms.

Instead, she said, "I've been thinking a lot about what would drive a person to enslave another. Were you lonely? Did you need help around the farm? I just don't understand it."

Ebba's smile was calculated to wound. If Rania hadn't grown up with a queen as a grandmother, she might have been laid low by it.

"I imagine there's quite a lot that little brain of yours doesn't understand," the witch scoffed. "As for that creature, feeding my magics with its life force is an honor above its station."

Rania's eyes sparked. "That was definitely *not* the right answer."

With a gesture towards the sea, a Nixie wave crashed over Ebba, drenching her and relieving her of the treasure. The knife, however, remained clutched in her hand. She spit words at Rania as she raised the blade above her head.

"How are you doing that? I sense no magic in you. No matter; give me my sealskin or face my blade."

Rania took off the pearl necklace and threw it to a Nixie. Instantly, her skin started to return to its natural color. She stood with her feet in the surf- blue-skinned and beautiful- churning the water and drawing still more Nixies to her side.-

"What sort of an abomination are you?"

"The kind that is about to teach you a lesson."

Movement down the beach drew both their attention. It was Kai and the selkie maiden walking towards them.

"Don't you dare show that creature the skin. I swear I'll kill you both."

Ebba started moving the knife in intricate patterns in the air while chanting words Rania didn't understand.

"I don't want trouble," Rania said, motioning for the Nixies to disappear.

The witch's eyes had started to glow. As the knife sliced through the air, the selkie maid collapsed to the rocks and started convulsing.

"Take it!" Rania screamed, throwing the skin at the witch's feet. "Just stop hurting her!"

The witch stopped her chanting and lunged to grab the pelt. It didn't take long for her to realize the skin was old and dusty, but it was enough time for Kai to show the Selkie her true skin, hidden in a beached boat.

Recovering from the magical attack, the Selkie hugged the beloved skin to her, slipped it on, and disappeared beneath the waves.

Ebba took a faltering step forward, and then she saw the seals, all of them swimming towards the shore with malice in their eyes. That's when she ran.

22

A Different Kind of Dancing

The air was brisk, but hundreds of brazier fires dotted the hillsides that surrounded the dancing pavilion. Pahl stood warming his hands at one near the row of royal tents. Besides a few people bustling about making sure all the lanterns were lit, he was by himself.

When a trumpet sounded, he startled and then laughed nervously at himself as the king was announced.

The royal attendants bustled about their sovereign as he made his way to the elaborate festival throne. Once seated, he shooed them away and motioned for Pahl to join him.

"I won't pretend," he began without preamble, "that I was happy when you presented me with that golden apple, but you have also brought me a prize beyond price, and for that, I am forgiving."

The king stared at the mapmaker before going on.

"The Princess Linnea was quite beautiful and charming at dinner. I am glad that I will soon have her in my arms. I hope she is skilled in the art of dance."

"No doubt, Sire," Pahl mumbled into the pause that followed.

Apparently satisfied with this response, the King continued.

"I've called you here before the others arrive to discuss some particulars. I will begin the dance with the Princess Astrid. Soon after, you and the Princess Linnea will join us. After a short interval, we will exchange partners so that you and Astrid can have your first dance as a betrothed couple."

Another pause spurred Pahl to say, "As you wish, Your Majesty."

"And I suppose," the king went on, "that I must give you one of my outer provinces to rule since I cannot have my daughter living above a map shop."

Pahl blanched. He had no interest in ruling anything.

"What is keeping them?" the king growled. "How long does it take for ladies to change into dancing slippers?"

Pahl volunteered to check on them but was spared the task as Astrid crested the hill, leading a long line of elegant ladies.

Linnea, who came behind Astrid, had a perfect view of the moment Pahl saw his future bride. In that instant, Linnea promised herself that she would only get married if she could find someone to look at her in that way.

The line of ladies was almost to the dance floor when the knights and princes who had participated in the competition arrived. All eyes were on the king as he led his youngest daughter to the glowing pavilion.

Pahl offered Linnea his arm. "You know," he said, "you could have told me that you were a princess with a magical horse."

Linnea laughed, "And ruin the surprise? Where's the fun in that? Besides, with the state I was in, would you have believed me?"

"Perhaps not. Well, maybe I would have believed the princess part, but I never would have guessed that Bert was magical."

Linnea snickered and turned to watch Astrid and the King.

"I'm afraid," Pahl went on, "that the king wants us to join them and then change partners so he can dance with you."

Linnea's shudder had nothing to do with the cool air. "I'm not sure how long my legs will hold up, but I'll do my best."

She paused for a moment, and then added, "Astrid seems to think I'm in danger. Is she just being over-cautious?"

"No," Pahl said, "the danger is real, but Astrid has a plan for sneaking you away tonight."

He and Astrid had meant to make their excuses not long after the dancing began, but once they were in each other's arms, all else was forgotten.

Linnea loved to dance. When she was young, she told her sisters that she would rather dance than eat. This night was different.

The king was a very fine dancer, but his fingers grasped a little too long, and his eyes wandered in a way that made her skin crawl.

It was well into the night before Linnea was able to get away.

She stood at one of the outer fires, enjoying the momentary solitude. As she took a deep breath, she closed her eyes and imagined a Breeze playing with her hair. She smiled, and when she opened her eyes she realized it wasn't her imagination. Two Breezes, her Fullanda Breezes, blustered around her excitedly.

It took her a moment to realize they were the Breezes she had sent to look after her sisters.

"Why are you here?" she asked in a panic, "Did you find them? Are they safe?"

The Breezes nodded enthusiastically. The first started acting out Rania stalking Linnea and then getting thrown into a pine tree. Linnea laughed. "You found Rania?" she asked. The Breeze nodded enthusiastically and then pantomimed a giant serpent.

"She's in pain? No, no, she lost her arms? Ok, sorry, that's just silly. Let me see... oh, I get it- she's going after that big, mean thingy that's guarding the lake in the far north!"

The Breezes looked at each other and then nodded.

"Thank goodness, I wasn't looking forward to that one."

Linnea turned to the other Breeze. "And do *you* know where Sylvi is headed? Is she with Rania, or did she decide to keep heading towards the troll castle?"

The Breeze nodded and pantomimed a troll.

"So that leaves me with... what was it???"

The Breezes conferred with each other. As one flew onto the other's shoulders, Linnea's face lit up.

"Giants!" she yelled. "Thank the stars the two of you were paying attention."

The Breezes disappeared suddenly. Before Linnea could turn, she felt a hot hand on her bare arm.

"Here you are," the king purred. "It's time to close out the dancing."

Linnea fixed on her best royal smile before letting him lead her back into the crowd.

23

Literary Wiles

Boots ushered Sylvi into the large castle courtyard.

"The kitchens are this way," he said. "It's warmer in there and I can grab us some things to snack on as we talk."

"Don't you need to hang your laundry?" she asked him.

Boots sighed. "You are quite right. They'll wrinkle if I leave them in the basket too long."

Without dropping Sylvi's arm, he steered them back the way they had come, picked up the laundry basket with his free hand, and nestled it on his hip for easier transport.

The drying rack was set up on the far side of the courtyard, away from the main gate. Boots found Sylvi a chair and talked to her as he hung the oversized clothing.

"Now, in all seriousness, how can I help you? I'm guessing that you are lost and need shelter or directions, but this is not a safe place to stay. We need to get you well and away before sundown."

"I was in earnest when I said that I'm here on business," said Sylvi. "My mother is ill, and there's a story, where I come from, of a healing crown that no longer works because your troll...."

"I wouldn't call him *my* troll," Boots interrupted.

"*This* troll, then," Sylvi amended, "traded a princess in exchange for one of the mystical stones that had powered the crown."

"Oooh," Boots said, momentarily forgetting his washing, "that sounds like a *really* good story. Will you tell it to me properly? No, wait, we need to get you out of here- well and away by sundown!"

"The sun just came up," Sylvi argued. "We have plenty of time. Why don't I tell you the story, and then we'll see if you can help me. It *is* a very good story."

Boots' resolve crumbled. "This is not good; not good at all. You already know my fatal weakness. Let me just finish hanging these up, and we can get comfortable in the parlor. Stories are always easier to remember if I can close my eyes and picture them. Besides, I want to be a good audience and give you all of my attention."

"That'll be something new," Sylvi laughed. "My sisters *never* pay attention when I'm telling them a story."

Boots looked mortally offended. "How dreadfully rude!"

"Oh, no," Sylvi backpedaled, "It's fine. I'm not a very good storyteller. I'll probably put you to sleep."

Boots looked her in the eye. "Why do I doubt that? But, honestly, I could use a good rest, so I'm fine either way."

It didn't take him long to finish hanging the laundry since only one giant undershirt and several socks could fit in the basket.

Soon, Sylvi found herself cozied up in an over-stuffed chair while Boots lay on the divan.

"This is perfect," he said. "Lady, please begin."

Sylvi cleared her throat and started at the beginning. "Once, not long ago, a great queen ruled in the land of Fullanda."

Boots sighed contentedly, and Sylvi smiled as she continued.

"The kingdom was prosperous and peaceful until the day a mysterious illness crept in. No one knew from whence it came, or, more importantly, how to send it on its way. It was merciless, for, though it did not act quickly, its end was universally fatal. Soon, it seemed, half the kingdom lay dead or dying, including the queen's own beloved husband."

Sylvi peered over at Boots, wondering if he really had fallen asleep. When his eyelid twitched, she decided it was safe to continue.

"Now, the queen came from an ancient and magical family. Long ago they had imbued precious stones with great power to help their kingdoms prosper. In her desperation and grief, the queen called on her extended kin to loan her their stones. She believed that once bound together, the gems could deliver them from their malady. Her family set themselves to the task, but none could bind the stones. One by one, they left the queen, but she would not give up. She worked without rest, and when, at last, she lay exhausted to the bone, a whisper away from death herself, a talisman as powerful as it was beautiful dazzled in the morning light. The queen had forged a crown to bind the four powers together. The crystal of cognizance was clear with straight, sharp lines; the blue of the spirit stone rivaled that of the heavens, and the gem of embodiment was rounded and smooth, the color of your innermost heart. The fourth stone was included as an afterthought. The stone of serenity wasn't just one hue, but danced with the colors of the Aurora itself. It was the power stone of Fullanda and was only added at the last minute to halt the progress of the disease until the other three could do their work. Little did anyone suspect that it would prove to be the most important in the end."

Boots jumped up so quickly that Sylvi gave a little yelp.

"So sorry," he said. "I just love a good ending, especially when the storyteller is a virtuoso like you."

Sylvi laughed and tried to push off the compliment. Finally, she said, "But that's not the ending," in order to distract him.

With an effort, Boots lay back on the divan and closed his eyes.

"I'm ready. Please continue," he whispered.

Sylvi took a sip of tea and continued. "In no time, the king was restored to full health, and the plague was eradicated, but it wasn't long before people started doubting that the crown was the cause of their rescue. Many of the healers and magic folk of the land swore that they were the real saviors. It was then that the kingdoms who had loaned their stones of power noticed an abnormal number of storms, failed crops and other disasters. They sent desperate word to Fullanda to return their treasures with haste. The queen immediately dismantled the crown and sent her own brothers to return the borrowed gems, while the stone of serenity remained in the crown and in Fullanda, looking for all the world like an innocent adornment."

Boots waited a good thirty seconds before opening one eye and asking, "Was *that* the end?"

Sylvi smirked. "Oh, no. There's *much* more, but that's all we have time for if we're going to get me 'well and away by sundown.' "

"You know full well that you've lured me in with your literary wiles, so no gloating," Boots mock-lectured her. He couldn't keep the stern demeanor for long. "I just have *so* many questions, but most importantly, which stone is it, the one that's supposed to be here?"

"The gem of embodiment," she replied.

"I knew it! I mean, I had a feeling it was that one, not sure why, it just seemed right. He traded it for love, right, the prince?"

Boots didn't wait for an answer, his brain was on fire. "I've been doing some research on the people who lived here before the troll, fascinating stuff- a real mystery. Do you think it was their odious princess, the one who lived here, that he traded the stone for, or do you think the troll got rid of the whole initial royal family and found a princess from somewhere else? Maybe if we look through some of those materials we can find a clue to any mysterious hiding spots in the castle."

He grabbed Sylvi's hand and started dragging her down the hall, then stopped abruptly, causing her to run into him.

"If we're not getting you away, our top priority has to be finding a place to hide you while the troll is at home. The far tower might work. He's too big to fit up the stairs. It's where I stayed when I first got here, so I didn't set off his allergy to the smell of humans. Now that he's used to my smell I've moved to the tower closest to the kitchens. It saves time."

Boots led her in the opposite direction, back across the sitting room through a small door and down a long stone passageway.

Sylvi had grown up in a castle, but it was bright, clean and filled with people. Most of the walls were painted light colors, and there were great tiled stoves in all of the rooms. This castle was all dark wood and stonework- a labyrinth of lonely halls and staircases, and Sylvi loved it.

The area they now traveled through was plain and unadorned. She guessed it had been a servant's passageway. Doors seemed to pop up at random, unlike the symmetry of her castle in Fullanda. After a sudden turn, several short staircases, and a jaunt through a room filled with armor, they came to a spiral staircase. Light streamed in through small round windows and so did the frigid air. Sylvi shivered.

"I forgot how drafty it can get up here. Please let me know if you don't think you'll be comfortable. I'll bring up more blankets, but we can always try the cellar if this is too cold."

The stairs were so tight a circle that Sylvi started to get dizzy. At last, they were at the top.

The large circular room had a high peaked wooden roof with long thin windows in the walls, except for the spot where a gigantic fireplace stood. Boots bustled over to it. "Oh, good, I left plenty of firewood. I'll get that started for you."

A four-poster bed with heavy curtains had been pushed near the fireplace, along with a circular rug, an overstuffed chair and a small table piled high with books. Sylvi sighed contentedly.

24

When Land & Sea Walk Together

Rania longed to jump into the waves and get as far away from the island as possible. She turned and took a step into the water, but a small cough stopped her.

"Were you going to leave without saying goodbye?" Kai actually sounded hurt.

"Aren't you coming with me? I thought your taste for lemmings would decide it if my companionship wasn't enough for you."

"I would move mountains for lemmings and your company," he said, "but, alas, I am still no swimmer. I fear I would drown before I got much of either."

"Don't be so dramatic." Rania smiled as she gestured to Ebba's small boat. "We can't leave the witch with easy transportation, and the Nixies said they could use it to give you a ride."

Kai pranced to the boat and jumped in. As the Nixies introduced themselves, Rania slowly walked back up the shore to the decoy seal skin. Sadness welled up in her as she touched it.

Neither she nor Kai had wanted to go back to the cave, but the subterfuge worked. It had bought them enough time for the Selkie to escape.

As Rania turned back to the waves, the Selkie Queen swam up to her. Rania handed her the skin. She took it gently in her mouth and carried it out to sea.

Rania dove in and swam up to the boat, which was already following the selkie pod.

"Ready to take on a lindworm?" she asked Kai.

"I thought you were in charge of the lindworm, and I was in charge of lemming retrieval."

"Sounds good to me," she said, diving under and savoring the joy of the water on her skin.

The pod wasn't headed to the island where Rania had met them, but one further north. As the sun began to set, they reached its shore. All the selkies but one removed their skins and danced in celebration. Some of the pod had arrived earlier and prepared a feast and lit a dozen small fires.

The Nixies landed Kai's boat deftly on the beach, and he thanked them kindly.

"They're good fun," he told Rania as she drew the boat further up on land.

The Nixies waved to Kai and then disappeared under the waves.

Rania laughed. "They like you. That doesn't happen often."

"Are you saying I'm not generally likable?" he asked with a foxy smirk.

"Stop fishing for compliments," she replied, tipping him out of the boat onto the pebbled beach.

The fires danced invitingly in the growing darkness. The Selkie Queen motioned Kai and Rania to join her at the largest.

"You have done us a great service. Tomorrow, we will fulfill our end of the bargain and take you to the Lindworm's island. But for tonight- enjoy the feast and be merry."

Rania held back a yawn. "I hate to say it, but I don't think I have enough left in me for merry-making tonight. Is there a place I can get some sleep?"

The Selkie Queen motioned to a grassy spot at the top of a small hill. "Some of the sisters have brought you warm human things to wrap up in since we've noticed that you don't have a fine layer of blubber to keep you warm."

Rania wondered if she should be offended in some way, but instead, she said, "Thank you. Um, before I go, can I just ask... do you know where the um, extra, sealskin came from; who it belonged to? Do you know about the... um, cave?"

The Selkie Queen seemed to deflate, and Rania noticed her great dark eyes take on an extra shine in the firelight.

"Yes, I do, but let us not speak of it tonight. After we deliver you to your destination, we will think of retribution. Tonight is for celebration."

As if on cue, a raucous tune reached their ears from a nearby fire where maidens danced holding hands.

"Fair enough," Rania said, "then I'll be off to bed. You coming, Kai?"

The fox shook his head. "Not yet. I'll be up soon."

Rania stretched as she lumbered up the hill. "Suit yourself. Goodnight."

When she was out of earshot, the Selkie Queen gave Kai a shrewd look. "Well, my arctic friend, what reward would you have for your bravery and kindness? Karina, the selkie you rescued, tells of how you were her only friend in her captivity and of how you led her to her skin in the end. It is within our power to lift your enchantment."

"No!" Kai blurted out. "I mean, I appreciate the offer, I truly do, but I love being a fox. I only... is there any way you could give me the ability to speak to other foxes? I get a bit lonely, and humans don't usually," he paused and glanced over to where Rania seemed to be making herself some sort of nest with the blankets the selkies provided, "take kindly to animals who speak their language."

"I could do this," the Selkie Queen replied, "but you would lose the ability to speak and understand the human tongue, and I do not believe you are quite ready for that. Am I correct?"

They both glanced over at Rania.

"You are."

Moments passed in silence as they watched the flames. Kai was trying to phrase a question that had been niggling at the back of his brain.

"I don't suppose, if someone wanted it, you could, um, transform them into another animal?"

The Selkie Queen laughed, but not unkindly. "I suppose I should be polite and pretend that I think you are asking about changing yourself into something bigger, or perhaps something that can fly, but I think I know your heart. It is not an easy road when the land and sea walk together, but with some brave souls, the results can be magical."

She motioned to the scene before them- selkies swimming in the water and dancing on the beach. If a fox could blush, Kai would have shone scarlet.

"What you have proposed," continued the queen "is but one solution to your dilemma. Walk a while more together and see what else you learn. Your reward will be waiting. We selkies don't forget when we are indebted."

And with that, she left him to watch the fire as she strode off to dance with her sisters.

Kai sat there for a while longer, then trotted up the hill and found a nice warm spot to sleep nestled up to Rania's back.

25

Sisters & Subterfuge

At last, the dancing was over, and Linnea walked back to the tents with Astrid and her sisters. They giggled excitedly as they went, talking over all the night's events.

Astrid and Pahl walked holding hands, her head resting on his shoulder.

Linnea was exhausted. When she stumbled, one of Astrid's sisters caught her arm and wrapped it in hers companionably as they walked.

"I'm Annalisa. You're a very good dancer."

"Thank you," Linnea replied. "You are, too. Who was the man in the red coat? The two of you schottische beautifully together."

"You're so kind," Annalisa said, blushing. "That's the duke of Valland. He's not who my father would like me to marry, but Astrid has given us all hope."

Linnea had never been more grateful that her grandparents wouldn't dream of forcing a marriage on her. Her own mother had never married, even though she was heir to the throne.

"Wait," Linnea said, looking around, "isn't that Astrid's tent down there?"

Annalisa laughed. "It's not quite time for sleep yet. We have a tradition of all gathering in Annika's tent at the end of the festival. She's our eldest sister, so hers is the largest. The men go off to discuss affairs of state and other lofty things, or so they tell us, and we sisters gather to talk about them."

Before the ladies could enter the large crimson tent, the king and his entourage approached.

"Girls, I bid you a good night. I expect that you won't keep our lovely guest up too late with your chatter. I will see you *all* in the morning." His eyes roved over Linnea suggestively before he swaggered off with the rest of the courtly men. After a few paces, he stopped and looked back.

"Mapmaker!" he bellowed. "Why don't you join us? You'll need some instruction on how to be a ruler of men if my outer provinces are soon to be yours."

The courtiers sneered with ill-disguised laughter as Pahl pulled himself away from Astrid.

"Father," said the tallest of the sisters, "might we keep him for a bit? The girls would like to instruct him on how to be the bridegroom of a princess. We shan't keep him long."

Her deep curtsey was elegant and respectful.

"A *man* with my daughters alone in the night; I am ashamed that you would suggest something so scandalous."

"Begging your pardon, Your Royal Father, but I hardly view the old mapmaker's son as a *man*. He was always with his venerable father, our tutor, as we were growing up, so we think of him quite as our own. It is a silly whim of ours, to give him a rite of passage. We can defer to another day, if that is your will."

The king seemed irritated but couldn't resist this further insult to the man he deemed unworthy of his daughter.

"Very well, Annika," the king conceded, "but make sure you get him to us in one piece." The king laughed heartily at his own joke, so the rest of the assembled joined in.

In keeping with the jest, Annika replied, "I give no promises, Your Majesty, but I'll do my very best," and all the ladies gave their father elegant curtsies goodnight.

A guard held the tent flap for them as they entered Annika's temporary living quarters. Several of the sisters waved and giggled at the guards as they drew Pahl in and closed the flap behind them.

The instant they were alone, the girls' frivolous manner dropped away. Making silent hand gestures at each other, they fanned out to precise positions within the tent.

All around the edges, the ladies clustered in twos and threes, giggling and gossiping loudly. Linnea felt Astrid grab her hand and drag her into a makeshift fort in the middle of the tent made of changing screens and blankets.

Annika, Annalisa and Pahl sat on the ground looking over what seemed to be a whole stack of maps.

"We can talk in here," Astrid whispered. "They shouldn't be able to hear us as long as we're not too loud. You've already met Pahl and Annalisa. This is my eldest sister, Annika."

Annika smiled kindly and motioned for Linnea to take a seat.

"Annalisa's a master of geography, and I'm our best strategist," Annika said. "The plan is to get you and the newly betrothed couple out tonight, but you need to tell us where you're headed, so we can come up with a plan. Oh, and Pahl, you're going to have to make this look good, so the guards don't suspect anything and report back to the king."

"What does that mean?" he asked with a look of fear in his eyes.

The side of Annika's lip twitched as three of her younger sisters appeared suddenly to grab Pahl and pull him into the outer room. As they started removing his outer garments, Linnea thought his shrieks might not have been acting.

"Now that we've got that settled," said Annika, "let's get to it."

"The only thing I know," said Linnea, "is that my great, great, maybe some more greats in there, uncle stopped at a city of giants somewhere in the northern part of the southern continent and was never seen again," said Linnea.

"Well, that's lucky," Annalisa replied. "You couldn't have planned it better if you had come here on purpose. Gyldenfare is at the far northern coast of the southern continent, and the Great Giant City is just over the mountains from here."

"But the giant city is abandoned, Annalisa," Astrid pointed out.

"It's abandoned *now*," Annalisa countered before turning to Linnea. "How long ago was this? If it was more than sixty years ago, he could have been there before the gods banished the giants back to Jottenheim."

"That seems right," Linnea said, starting to get excited. "Maybe he was there before they were banished. He disappeared after going there. Is it possible he went with them to Jottenheim?"

Annika's eyebrows knit together in concentration. "We'll get you to the ruins. You can look for the stone or any evidence of your uncle. If that fails, you'll have to call the North Wind."

"Excuse me?" Linnea said, hoping to all the gods that she hadn't heard the princess correctly.

"The North Wind. He's the only one who can get you to Jottenheim. He brings messages to and from the great eagle giant, Raesvelg," Annika explained.

Linnea felt faint. "Please tell me you made that up."

Astrid looked concerned. "Don't worry; he's wonderful, the North Wind. I'm sure he'll take you. We just need to think of a way to get his attention."

"Do you have any krumkake or any other sweets? I'm going to need dessert and a lot of humility," Linnea said with a grimace.

Astrid laughed. "That sounds like a story. You'll have to tell us the whole tale when we have more time."

"Annalisa," Annika said, "get a map together for them. I'll have Anya add krumkake to the supply list and tell Pahl the plan. He'll have to meet you there." Pahl poked his overly made-up face into the fort. "Did I hear my name? Please tell me this can be over soon."

Annalisa and Annika had the decency to refrain from laughing, but Astrid burst out into great guffaws.

Pahl rolled his eyes and tried to ignore her while Annika explained the plan.

"You need to leave here looking utterly angry at your treatment and storm off towards home to sulk and get cleaned up. Do you think you can get to Linnea's magic horse?

"That shouldn't be a problem."

"Oh, good," Linnea said. "I was worried we might have to leave Bert behind."

"Get the horse," Annika went on, "And anything you can't live without and make your way to the Great Giant City. Astrid and Linnea will meet you there."

"Shouldn't we travel together?" Pahl asked. It's a two-day ride through the gap, and there have been thieves about."

"It's safer if you're not seen together. Now go, and don't forget to look angry. We need the guards to report back that you are in disgrace and won't be joining the men tonight. The longer before they start to look for you the better."

The sisters gave Astrid and Pahl some space to say goodbye, then pushed him out of the tent where he did a very good job of fuming in disgraced outrage.

"And now, Linnea," said Annika, "I have to ask you a very important question. Can you keep a secret?"

Linnea thought back to all the times she had tattled on her sisters and said, with as straight a face as she could muster, "Absolutely."

Annika's eyebrow raised one millimeter, and Linnea broke. "Alright, I don't know if I can keep a secret. Some things are dangerous *not* to tell, but I'd like to believe that I can hold my tongue when it's really important."

Annika stared at her for a moment, and then nodded.

"We've never told anyone what we're about to tell you. Our father will be furious when he finds the three of you missing. He is a ruthless man. We must send you down a road he cannot travel."

Linnea must have looked worried because Annalisa put a hand on her arm.

"Don't worry. *You* will be safe. Annika, why don't you go see Anya about the supplies? I'll show Astrid which exit they need to use."

26

A Storyteller's Tale

Boots got the fire in the tower room roaring.

"We should bring up a few more armfuls before nightfall," he said, eyeing the wood pile. "But before that, I need to get the lamb roast in the oven and find you some food. You really look like you could use a good meal. Come on."

And with that, he put the grate in front of the fire and headed down the stairs. It took Sylvi a moment to realize that she should follow him.

Once in the kitchen Boots put on an apron and started pulling out pots, pans and all sorts of foods. Sylvi's mouth started watering just looking at it all.

"That's the one thing about living with a troll. You'll never go hungry. Trolls really like their food. We've got sheep and pigs; then there are the goats and cows for milk and cheese and chickens for eggs, of course. That's where he goes each day- to the farm. I just have to mind the chickens and let him know when the vegetables and preserves in the root cellar are getting low."

Without pausing, Boots slid a tray over to Sylvi. It was filled with biscuits, slices of ham, a slab of butter and several open jars. Sylvi peered into one and sniffed.

"That one is lingonberry jam. The others are honey and pickled herring. I don't recommend putting them together. And here's the coffee," he said, handing her a steaming cup. "That should hold you until I get the dinner going."

Watching Boots in the kitchen was mesmerizing. Sylvi almost forgot to eat- until she smelled the coffee. How long had it been since she had had coffee???"

"Where did you learn to cook like this?" She asked with a mouth full of buttery ham biscuit.

"The life of a storyteller isn't all inns and fancy houses. My master and I spent a lot of our days on the road. He believed in eating well, so he took spices and delicacies as payment when he could get them."

"Did you miss your family when you were on the road?" she asked.

"Well," Boots answered while seasoning a lamb roast, "I don't really remember my birth family. The old master heard me singing to myself as I was mucking out the goose pen for the minister who had taken me in when my parents and brothers died. The minister was nice enough but had eight children of his own to feed and was happy that I would be learning a trade. I was nervous," he went on, putting the roast in the oven and tossing another log in the fire, "about leaving the town I had spent my whole life in, until I heard the old master that night in the town hall. He could weave a spell with his words that made the whole tale unfold right before your eyes. We left the next day. I was seven years old, and since then have been all around the Northern Kingdoms."

"Have you been to Fullanda?" Sylvi asked.

"Fullanda was beautiful: lush forests and crystal blue lakes. That's where you're from?" he asked, refilling her coffee before chopping the vegetables.

Sylvi nodded.

"How on earth did you get this far to the northeast on your own and on foot?" he asked in wonder.

"I wasn't on my own. Not at first, anyway. My sisters-"

"The horrible ones that don't listen to your stories," Boots cut in.

Sylvi laughed. "The very ones. We took a small ship to the mouth of the Varm River. There was a storm, and we were separated."

Boots just stared at her. "You mean to tell me that you traveled the entire Westerback Forest on your own and made it here in one piece? I was mistaken when I said you should be well and away by dinner. A troll will be nothing after what you've seen."

Sylvi couldn't tell if he was teasing her.

"Yes, the rabbits and deer were quite fierce."

"Is that all you saw, truly? The forest is supposed to be haunted with all sorts of angry spirits, not to mention the Nacken." Boots shuddered. "I came the easy way- down the road from the north."

Sylvi laughed. "Someone's been telling you tales. I didn't see any angry spirits, just some cordial animals, some helpful mushrooms, and a lonely man with a violin."

"Funny," Boots chuckled, "Just a man with a violin."

"He gave me this flower," Sylvi said, taking it out of her satchel.

Boots actually flinched away from the plant. "The Nacken gave you one of his magical water lilies? You truly are *not* a woman to be trifled with."

"No," Sylvi said, chuckling awkwardly, "that's my sister, Rania. I'm nobody. I'm just trying to blend in."

"Well, you're doing a very bad job of it."

Sylvi's blush reached all the way to the tips of her ears.

After a delicious lunch, Boots took her to the library. It wasn't as grand as the one in Castle Fullanda, but it had all sorts of cozy reading spots and tables for taking notes.

Sylvi was tempted to peruse the shelves and curl up in a particularly inviting window seat, but Boots dragged her to a far corner.

"This is where they keep all the castle records. I thought we could start by looking for anything related to the construction of the castle. We might find a mention of hidden passages or treasure chambers."

He took several thick volumes off a low shelf and brought them to the nearest table.

"Now, the troll hasn't forbidden me to go into any mysterious rooms, and I haven't found anything suspicious in my previous wanderings. Of course, I wasn't looking for anything as specific as we are now, so I could have walked past it each day on my way to do the washing and never thought anything of it."

Boots brought over a ladder that would have looked more at home beside a wood shed and leaned it against the high shelves. Deftly hiking up his skirts with one hand, he climbed up and started pulling out more books and scrolls. Dust rained down on Sylvi as he handed them down to her.

When he was done, they brought them all to the table and began sorting through their finds. Most of the journals were lists of supplies ordered or payroll to staff, but occasionally, they would come across a drawing of some exquisite stonework or an order for something completely absurd.

"What do you think they wanted the twenty-five weasel tunics for?" Sylvi asked.

"Presumably for their children, who had all been turned into wild animals by a disgruntled sorceress," Boots replied, and they spent the rest of the afternoon making up the story of the Weasel Princes while digging through more books.

"I have got to add this story to my repertoire," Boots laughed, "but don't worry; I'll give you credit as co-creator. My master was great at making up new tales, but he'd always pass them off as being handed down to him. I suppose it gave them more credibility. Either that or he could shrug it off more easily if nobody liked them."

"Where is your master now?" asked Sylvi.

"He passed on about two years ago now," Boots answered.

"I'm sorry," Sylvi apologized.

Boots' wan smile held a multitude of untold emotions. "Don't be," he finally said. "He had a good and long life, doing what he loved. He was a fine man and a true friend. I'm glad for every moment I had with him. You know," he went on, a gleam lighting his eye, "he would have loved this new adventure, though his bushy white beard would have been hard to explain on a princess."

Sylvi snorted at the image.

"Well," Boots said, picking up a stack of books, "I think we can put these back." He climbed the ladder and started re-shelving them. "No real leads yet, but if it takes all year, we'll find it!"

At the look on Sylvi's face, he apologized. "Oh, no, I'm *so* sorry. I completely forgot that we're doing this to save your mother. Please forgive my glib comment. How much time do we have?"

Sylvi blinked rapidly and turned pages of a hefty tome as she answered.

"I'm not quite sure. I've been marking the days since we left on my bracelet, but I don't know how accurate it is. Time moved… differently in the forest."

"See!" Boots said, "I told you it's haunted! What does your bracelet say?"

Sylvi did a quick tally of the marks. "It looks like I've been traveling for about twenty-eight days, which would make this October 14th or 15th."

"Close- it's the twenty-first," Boots corrected.

"That's not close," Sylvi protested, panic welling. "How could I have lost almost a week?"

"You said it yourself," Boots said as he sat down next to her, "that forest plays with your mind. Some have been lost in it for years. How long does that leave us?"

"They'll wake her on November 11th, so that only leaves twenty-one days."

"And the return journey will take another twenty-eight...?" Boots finished with dread in his voice.

"Oh, no; my grandfather gave me a ring that will transport me back. We can still make it."

"That's quite a gift! What kind of man is your grandfather?"

Sylvi didn't know why she shied away from this opportunity to tell Boots her true identity. Maybe she just didn't want things to change between them.

"He's an explorer and a scholar," she said, truthfully enough. "I don't have a father, but I never really thought about it because my grandfather was always there for me."

"You're lucky. Horrid sisters and sick mother aside, it sounds like a nice life. And you're right; we still have time. If the stone is here, we'll find it."

"Thank you," said Sylvi.

"Think nothing of it, m'lady," Boots said, tipping his head to her, "I only ask for the exclusive composition rights to the tale of your epic quest."

"Granted," said Sylvi, smiling.

"I'll hold you to that!" Boots said as a booming noise from down the hall caused him to nearly fall from his chair in surprise. It took Sylvi a while to realize that the sounds were actually words.

"GUUUNHIIIILDAAAAHHHH!!! WHERE ARE YOU?!?! AAAAACHOOOO!"

27

A Farewell to Friends

Kai was surprised when Rania climbed into the boat after packing the last load of gear.

"You're not swimming with the rest of the crew?" he asked.

"I can change my mind if you were looking forward to some alone time," she replied, raising an eyebrow.

"No, I enjoy your company. I just thought you'd prefer to be in the water."

"I did offer to help push the boat, but the Selkie Queen said that I need to keep up my strength for the trip across the ice and, of course, the encounter with the Lindworm," Rania said as she made space in the over-stuffed boat.

"I can't believe how much they think we'll need for our trip," she mumbled. "How am I going to carry all of this once we're on land?"

Kai found an empty spot near her, and they settled in for a long day at sea.

The Nixies who had pushed the boat the day before were back, and they had brought friends.

Soon, they picked up speed. The wind blowing through her hair felt marvelous and almost made up for having to stay dry.

Kai smiled and even let his tongue loll out of his mouth when he thought Rania wasn't looking.

It was a glorious day. The clouds rolled by, and a pod of curious dolphins swam up to take a look at the unlikely traveling companions.

"I wish I could help move the boat. I feel so guilty just sitting here," Rania said as the sun started setting.

"You're not just sitting here," Kai smiled. "You're keeping me company."

Rania laughed. "Well, I'm not doing a good job of that, either. I've barely said more than, 'doesn't that cloud look like a chicken' and 'how many dolphins do you count' all day."

"Good company isn't always about conversation," he said, then turned his head away from her. A few minutes later, he turned back. "I've been thinking. Maybe you *can* help move the boat."

"So you've realized I'm *not* good company, and you're finding me a new job?" she asked.

Kai chose to ignore her and went on. "I noticed when I was watching you swim that you seem to move the water away from yourself when you put on a burst of speed. I was thinking- maybe you could put your hands in the water and try propelling the boat in the same way."

A smile crept across her face. "So, you were watching me swim, were you?"

Kai was glad he couldn't blush. "If you're going to be like that," he said, "I will keep my ingenious observations to myself."

Rania laughed. "Hmmm, I hadn't really thought about it before. It's just the way I've always swam. I guess I do think about sending the water away from me; Might be worth giving it a go."

Tentatively, she leaned over and put a hand in the water. She bit her lip, scrunched up her face, and shot the water in such a strong stream that it spun the boat in circles.

It took a long time to convince the Nixies that this wasn't a fun new game. Kai looked a bit seasick by the time they were back on track.

Rania adjusted the gear and found a place facing backward in the exact center of the boat. If she used both hands she could get them going more or less straight ahead. Kai acted as the lookout, letting her know when the selkie pod was changing direction and helping her course correct.

"You are a genius!" she told Kai as they reached a small island for the night.

Their days soon fell into a pattern- ocean travel during the day and at night- warm food and talk, then sleep nestled with the seals for warmth.

The days were getting shorter and the nights colder as they traveled ever northward.

The only detour they had to make was when they saw orcas in the distance. Luckily, the whales kept heading south.

That night, Rania tramped back to the selkie camp carrying fallen branches to break into firewood. Kai followed, dragging an enormous branch behind him.

The selkies had stopped taking off their sealskins to conserve warmth, so it was a surprise when the Selkie Queen came to their fire in her human form.

She sat down on a rock, seal skin wrapped around her shoulders like a stole.

The rest of the selkies, all in seal form, jostled about on the rocky shoreline, settling in for the long night.

Rania turned the fish that had been cooking in the fire.

"This is the last island before the one you seek," the Selkie Queen told them, "and the Lindworm's land is not hospitable to trees."

"So, enjoy the fire while we can?" Rania asked.

The Selkie Queen smiled. "Indeed."

Rania could swim like a Selkie, but she couldn't catch and consume fish like they did in their seal forms. She would miss eating warm food, of course, but she had never minded dried meat and cracker bread. What she would miss most was the feeling she got when she had been foraging in the woods and saw the camp flames warm in the darkness. It helped to hold back the long nights.

Rania knew that the fish on her skewer would still be too hot to eat, but hunger prompted her to try it anyway. She burned her fingers and her tongue, but it was worth it. In these temperatures, nothing stayed warm for long.

The Selkie Queen was more patient and decided to talk while her food cooled to a more manageable temperature.

"When the seal told me you needed to find the Lindworm, I was skeptical of your success."

The pause that followed was bordering on rude.

"And now...?" Rania prompted.

"After seeing you confront that witch I am somewhat less concerned."

Rania scowled at her. "Your confidence in me is truly heartwarming."

The queen chuckled. "What you're proposing to do is no small thing, but if I did not believe you up to the challenge, I would talk you out of going. You *can* do this, but there will be suffering. You are one of my daughters now, and it is hard for a mother to send a child into danger. It warms my heart that, at least, I do not send you alone."

Kai was off finding one last branch for the fire. Rania watched his silhouette disappear into the darkness and realized that the Selkie Queen wasn't the only one whose heart was warmed by her companion.

"We will take you into the sea ice," said the queen, "but once it starts freezing together we must leave you. The boat has all the gear you should need, but navigation will be difficult. The sunstone we gave you can find its location, even in the grayest conditions, but only during the day. At this time of year, those hours are few."

Rania secretly thought that if this was supposed to be a pep-talk, the Selkie Queen could use some lessons.

"Besides the gear," she went on, "I have a gift for each of you."

Kai dropped the branch he was dragging into the firelight. He hadn't received many gifts since becoming a fox. In his meager experience, food scraps seemed to be most likely.

"Rania," said the Selkie Queen, "we have been concerned that you still have not developed a fine layer of blubber to keep you warm. We have decided to give you a special ointment that we use on our pups before their waterproof fur comes in. It will insulate you from the harshest cold. Be sure to apply it to your face in particular since you will need to leave at least your eyes exposed, and the scarves for your face aren't as warm as the rest of your gear."

Rania took the pot of salve and thanked the queen.

"And for our four-footed friend," the selkie went on, "I have remembered an ancient spell that might help with the wish we talked of earlier."

Kai fidgeted nervously. He wasn't sure which wish she was referring to and hoped she would be discreet in front of Rania.

"I can gift you the ability to understand the intentions of other animals. It will not allow you to speak with others of your kind, but it should bring you better understanding."

Kai wasn't sure if this gift was better than food scraps, but he thanked her kindly anyway.

In the morning, the Selkie Queen removed her seal skin again and walked over to the boat where Rania and Kai were making the last preparations to leave.

"Do you remember what I told you?" she asked.

Rania thought over the many instructions she had been given, knowing she had probably forgotten half of them.

"That white bears will take the easiest meal they can get?" she guessed.

The Selkie Queen chuckled. "No, I mean the part about the Lindworm."

Rania nodded. "I know what I have to do. I don't understand it, but I've been repeating the steps to myself each night so I don't forget."

"Very good, and never forget that you are part of our pod now, both of you," she added, giving Kai a significant look. "Don't forget, young fox, that we still owe you a favor. Find a seal or dolphin when you decide what you want from us. They will take us the message."

She leaned down and pressed her cheek to his in a traditional selkie leave-taking.

When she did the same with Rania, Rania pulled her into a hug.

"That's how humans say goodbye, well, when they like each other anyway," she said hastily.

All the other selkies decided that they wanted hugs. They took off their sealskins and pressed in for a proper farewell. Only one remained in her seal form. Rania hoped that her friend would trust enough to take it off again one day. She kneeled to hug the seal that had once been a captive.

"I hope we meet again under better circumstances," Rania said, and Karina, the selkie girl barked enthusiastically.

Kai turned to the Selkie Queen. "The gift! It works! I understood her intention. She agrees with you, Rania, wholeheartedly."

Kai was now certain that the selkie gift was much better than food scraps.

Rania finished loading the boat, hoisted Kai up and pushed out into the waves.

She realized with a jolt that the next land they touched would be on the island of the Lindworm.

It didn't take long for them to start seeing ice in the water. Most of it was in thin plates, but occasionally a small iceberg would drift silently by. By mid-day, they were getting much more frequent.

Rania knew that the selkies would leave them soon, and she tried hard to beat back the dread that came with the thought of their absence.

The Nymphs had offered to stay with Kai and her until they reached land, but Rania could see them becoming more sluggish the further north they traveled. When the selkies barked their last goodbyes and headed back south, Rania told the Nymphs that they should follow.

The Selkie Queen couldn't tell them how much ice there would be before they got to the island. If they were lucky, the plates wouldn't be fused together yet. In the gear was a long pole with a metal tip that they could use to break up thinner ice and deflect themselves around larger icebergs.

It was a bright clear day, making navigation easy. The boat had oars, but Rania preferred moving the water behind them with her hands. Because of the selkie salve, she could put them in the icy water for hours without feeling the cold.

"I'm worried about us floating off course in the night," Kai said, breaking the silence that had settled over them after the loss of their traveling companions.

This would be the first of what could be several nights at sea. With the pod gone the boat was feeling a lot smaller in the vast ocean.

"We can sleep in shifts," Rania said in a voice more confident than what she was feeling. "Wake me if you see us drifting too far off course."

Kai nodded.

Rania took a deep breath before speaking again; knowing that if he took her up on the offer she was about to make, it would be a lonely journey without him.

"It's not too late to turn back. I can take you to that last island. It seemed nice there."

She was going to say more, but Kai put his paw on her hand.

"We're in this together."

28

An Elaborate Escape

"Quick, take off your dress!"

Linnea wasn't sure which of Astrid's many sisters had made this curious demand, but she was glad when an explanation was given.

"We're going to switch places with Annalisa and Amelia because their tents are closest to the forest," Astrid said. "It will be easier to slip away from there."

As many hands helped Linnea strip off the ornate ball gown, Annika went into detail.

"We've become experts at masquerading as each other. That's another reason I wanted you and Annalisa to spend some time together. She'll be taking your place."

"But," Linnea protested, "I haven't had time to practice acting like her. Won't the guards notice?"

The whole room went up in giggles as Annalisa blushed.

"Once, when I was *much* younger," she said, "I passed out from all the dancing, and they couldn't wake me. As it's a mortal offense for a guard to touch a princess of the realm, four guards had to carry me to my tent in a bathtub."

Warming to the story, one of the younger girls picked up the narrative: "The next festival day, the guards had a special tub brought down with wheels attached. They call it the princess-cart."

This brought on more peals of laughter that Annika cut short.

"It's worked to our advantage. We've played it up so that we can hide any of us under her cloak in the tub and pretend to be asleep. You've been a trooper, Lisa."

Annalisa smiled and started putting on Linnea's dress.

"I'll need your bracelet, too, if we're to make it convincing," she said. "Everyone noticed it. Is it a talisman or something?"

Linnea looked at the leather wristband that Sylvi had made them. She had stopped marking days when she arrived in town but was reluctant to let it go, especially now that she was heading back into the unknown.

"It's for keeping track of time, so we know when we need to be home."

The lump in her throat stopped her from giving more detail.

"Amelia," Annika called, "Make a quick replica from the under flooring of the tent- it's about the same color. Annalisa is right; showing the bracelet will make her disguise more convincing, but Linnea must keep the original."

Annika's orders were always carried out immediately and without complaint. Linnea found herself wondering what it would be like to have sisters who actually did what you asked them to do.

To her surprise, she realized that she, Rania and Sylvi were so fiercely independent, because they had been given freedom and love in their childhood. These girls needed to be on their guard, living under the shadow of their father like they did. Relying on each other and hypervigilance had kept them safe over the years, but it hadn't been an easy life.

"It's time to get in the tub," Annika said, turning to Linnea.

As she clambered in, she noticed the sisters clustered around Astrid. They took turns hugging her and whispering final farewells. Silent tears ran down their faces as some of them tried to keep up the inane chatter for the sake of the guards. Annika was the last to hug her sister. Her eyes were dry, but Linnea thought she held on a bit longer than the others.

"May Freya light your way," was all she said before clapping Astrid on the shoulder and turning to the others.

Linnea didn't see the silent hand motions that called them all into action, since Astrid had thrown the cloak over her head. She did her best to pretend she was asleep as the guards were called to roll her to Annalisa's tent. When they got there, Astrid, in a frighteningly accurate Amelia impression, said, "Oh, just leave her over there. I've called for a maid to help me get her into her bed."

Linnea heard the guards leave, but it was some time before Astrid let her out of the tub.

"We would normally wait until the guards were getting sleepy, but we don't have time. We need to change into peasant outfits and slip out the back."

"But where are we going?" Linnea asked.

Astrid smiled. "Have you ever been to Faerie?"

29

The Troll who Sold His Princess for a Stone

"Guuunhiiildaaaaaahhh!" the Troll boomed. "Where are you, you lazy wretch?" And where is my COFFEEE?!?! I smell something...AHHCHOOOO!!!"

Boots' face had drained of all its color. "I lost track of time," he whispered frantically. "Quick, you've got to get back to the tower. He's blocking the fastest way, but if you take this back hallway and head up the last staircase on the left, you should find it. I'll head him off and buy you some time. I'll bring you food once he's asleep, but you have to promise me that you'll stay in the tower until I get there."

"GUUNHILDAAAAAHHHH!"

"Promise!"

Boots looked frantic, so Sylvi said, "I promise."

"Now go," he said as he pushed her out a small door at the back of the room and closed it behind her.

"You're awfully demanding, Princess Gunhilda," Sylvi said under her breath, smiling despite the danger.

She paused for a moment, trying to let her eyes adjust to the dark hallway. Behind the door she could hear Boots and the Troll.

"Why were you late? I called and called for you," the Troll said sulkily.

"I was merely trying to find a new story to sing for you tonight," said Boots in a falsetto that almost made Sylvi giggle. "Now let's get you back to the kitchen. I'll pour you some nice fresh coffee and finish up dinner. I made lamb roast tonight."

"Mmmm, lamb, my favorite. Ahhchooo! What is that smell? It is like maiden and flowers, eeehhch! You don't have a visitor?" he asked menacingly. "I said no humans but you!"

"No, no," Boots protested. "That pesky South Wind keeps blowing flowers down the chimney in here. Let's get you to the kitchen."

It took a moment for Sylvi to realize that she should be finding her way up to the tower. She tried to remember Boots' instructions as she fumbled down the dark hallway. It seemed to be slowly veering to the left, but though there were a lot of closed doors, she didn't see any stairs.

She was just about to start trying doors when a rickety staircase appeared on the right. Relieved to find any staircase at all, she started climbing it without thinking twice. It went up one story and ended in a small door.

After struggling to get it open, she realized that it had a bench in front of it on the other side. It was very dark, but once she was through, Sylvi could see a light at the end of a short hall.

The light was coming from a small balcony overlooking an enormous dining hall. It reminded her of the musician's gallery at Castle Fullanda.

She was about to go back to the staircase when she heard Boots bustling the Troll into the room below.

"Now sit here and drink your coffee while I get your dinner."

He ushered the Troll into a large chair at the head of the table and put a heavy tray laden with a mixing bowl full of coffee and a platter heaped with biscuits.

As quietly as she could, Sylvi turned and was starting to move back towards the door when she heard the Troll say, under his breath, "Silly princess, if you really *are* a princess."

She froze and decided to listen to see if she could hear more. If Boots was in danger, she needed to warn him.

It had been a while since she had camouflaged her skin; she was so used to keeping it peach to look more like the people of this part of the world, it took her a moment to remember how.

Once fully changed, she slowly lowered herself to the floor and crawled to the edge of the balcony to peek over.

The Troll was quite large this close up, but he drank his coffee with surprising delicacy.

He grumbled and laughed to himself, but Sylvi couldn't catch any of the words.

Soon, Boots was back, pushing a cart filled with food.

Sylvi's mouth watered as the smell of roast lamb and potatoes reached her.

"AHHCHOOO!" The Troll sneezed, again.

"That smell! It's just as bad in here. Are you sure a princess didn't sneak in? It smells just like a human princess!"

"That South Wind must have blown flowers down *this* chimney as well, even though it promised it would go far, far away."

Boots' eyes darted around the room as he served the Troll his food.

"You spoke to the South Wind and exhorted a promise from it?" the Troll asked. "I'm impressed, little one. I'll make a troll of you yet!"

Sylvi decided it was time to leave. As she began inching her way towards the staircase, something stopped her in her tracks- a lute being tuned.

Was Boots about to sing a story to the troll? If so, she really didn't want to miss it. The obedient little princess inside her head reminded her of the peril in staying. When this didn't get her moving her brain tried showing graphic images of what the troll might do if he found her in his castle.

This *did* get her moving, if at a snail's pace. She was less likely to be heard if she went slowly, right?

As she moved, the conversation from below filtered up over the balcony. "The South Wind told me an interesting story today," Boots said as he continued to tune his instrument. The troll just made contented noises as he devoured the food Boots had served him.

"It was about a troll who traded his princess for a stone," Boots went on. "It made me think, how do I know you won't sell *me* for a stone."

The troll belted out a deafening laugh.

"Because I wouldn't sell you for anything," he boomed. "I would give you away for the asking!"

His raucous laughter was punctuated with more sneezes.

"You're very funny," Boots said dryly. "What about that prince, though? What if he tries to steal his stone back?"

Sylvi's snail-like progress halted altogether as she strained to hear the troll's response.

"If I were a troll who had something of such value, I would hide it in such a way that only someone willing to give what it was worth could retrieve it- the only sensible thing to do, really."

The troll stopped talking as a new sneezing fit took him. When he recovered he went on. "And don't you go poking around trying to find treasure. If it were me, only a royal princess of the blood would do as payment, not just royalty by marriage, like you."

Boots finished tuning his lute and asked, "So what tale would you like me to sing you tonight?"

"Tell me of the mighty troll who sold his princess for a stone."

"It was just idle gossip from a flighty wind," Boots protested.

"You'll think of something," said the troll, pushing back his chair and taking out his pipe.

"Hmmm," said Boots, strumming some chords experimentally.

"Now the Troll has commanded – It is time for his song- and this night I will sing it- will you listen, my friend? For the tale is so haunting- the Troll fierce and wild- you had best stay a distance- will you brave it, my men?"

At the sound of Boots' voice all thought of going back to her room evaporated, and Sylvi's progress towards the stairs was lost. His voice was magical! She let it tug her back towards the balcony.

"For there's not just a troll- but a horrible princess- her voice was like birdies- her smell like a breeze. Now the troll knew the rules- that he must keep a princess- but the horrible truth is- that she made him sneeze."

As if on cue, the troll sneezed and then blew his nose, creating a sound like a trumpet. Sylvi jumped, but Boots kept singing.

"Now one day a brave hero- a knightly type figure- rode to the troll's doorstep- with a threat on his tongue. Give me the fair princess- said the insolent puppy- and the troll almost squashed him- right into the dung."

The troll gave an appreciative grunt then went back to puffing on his pipe.

"But he stopped and he thought- yes, I could squash this ingrate- but he saw there before him- a chance to be free. So he said, 'you may have her- for a rock or a pebble- on the promise you never- bring her back to me."

Sylvi's giggle floated down to them as Boots strummed the final chords of the song.

Fortunately, the troll was fast asleep in his chair, snoring like thunder.

Boots took the pipe and knocked out the ash in the fireplace before heading for the balcony. It didn't take him long to find Sylvi.

"I thought I heard you! What are you doing here? If he finds you... well, I don't have the skills to get blood out of rugs yet, so please, please, *please....*"

"Make sure I get caught in the courtyard?" Sylvi suggested, "Because field stones are easily cleaned?"

Boots stifled a laugh, and then sighed. "He really is dangerous, Sylvi. Why would you risk it?"

"I was lost and... and then I heard you sing," was her sheepish reply.

A smile crept across Boots' face. "My singing *is* worth risking death, it's true, but I am perfectly happy to sing for you at any time, risk free. And because you have such excellent taste, you are forgiven. Just, please, don't do it again. It really was needlessly dangerous."

30

Many Rather Large Creatures

It was hard for Kai to sit in the boat and let Rania do all the work.

"I'm not doing all the work," she assured him. "You're keeping us on course. I'm just the muscle."

But as he watched her breaking up ice with the pole for the third time that day, he wished he had a bit of muscle (and some hands) to help her out.

"There has got," Rania panted, "to be a better way to get to this Freyja-forsaken island."

She slunk to the bottom of the boat in utter exhaustion.

"Why couldn't I have some of my mother's powers?" Rania sulked. "She could do all sorts of things with fire. I bet she could blast a way through all this ice."

"Does she go around blasting things at home?" Kai asked.

Rania laughed. "No, she's usually lighting fires and warming up coffee that's gone cold, but I bet she *could* blast things if she wanted to."

Kai didn't know what to say. He was curious about this mother they were trying to save, but he knew it was a touchy subject. Besides, his own mother had been so cold and distant that he hadn't thought twice about leaving home when he was turned into a fox. He marveled at Rania's fierce love and open heart.

"Well, next time I travel to a frozen island to confront a malevolent beast," Kai said, "I'll be sure to take her instead of you."

"That sounds really good right now," Rania replied. "I'll take a nice long nap, and *she* can spend time with a sarcastic quadruped."

Kai smirked and went back to keeping watch. The ice chunks were thicker now. He scanned ahead for any danger, hoping desperately he would see land.

"Rania," he said a few minutes later," what do you think that is?"

He motioned his snout directly ahead of them. Rania leaned forward and squinted, trying to read the hazy whiteness in the distance.
"Is it...the island?" she asked without much hope in her voice.

"I don't think so," he replied.

"Is it a storm?" she whispered.

It was neither. Within minutes, they were completely surrounded by a cold, dense fog.

"Well, that's not good," Kai mumbled. "In case you were wondering."

He wanted to jump into Rania's lap, but he stayed where he was.

"I'm glad I'm just the muscle," she said with only a slight tremor. "Looks like the navigator has his work cut out for him."

Kai took a deep breath and thought hard.

"The sunstone!" he said. "It helps you navigate in bad conditions; where did we put it?"

"Ummm, with the gear?" Rania said unhelpfully.

Most of the gear was packed securely in the front of the boat; tightly tied down under an oilskin canvas. There were packs with food and water in the midsection that also had a canopy of canvas but were accessible for use. They lay on either side of a small space lined with thick lamb's wool and quilted blankets that they used for sleeping.

Kai could dig further into the gear but didn't have fingers to open crates or untie knots, so, yet again, he had to rely on 'the muscle' to do most of the work.

Rania wriggled into the small space and tried not to make a complete mess as she dug through the supplies, but her hands were shaking. Why in all the gods had she not simply put the stone in her satchel with the selkie balm? She knew that they would probably run into overcast skies or snow. Why was she always making dumb mistakes like this? Maybe she was only good for her ability to whack things. A litany of reproach circled in her mind as she fumbled blindly for the stone. She couldn't even remember the last time she saw it.

She was so absorbed in her fear that she didn't notice the warm furry body that had found its way in to lean against her.

"We'll find it," Kai said. "There's no immediate hurry. Why don't you go up top for a breath of cool air, and I'll nose about down here for a bit. I'll let you know when I need a break."

Rania nodded, grateful for his calm words and warm presence. Cool air sounded like just what she needed. She wormed her way out, then settled on a bench and tried to concentrate on her breathing. As she peered into the fog, however, something electrified her pulse- something was moving out there- something big, and it was headed their way.

"K...Kai?" she stammered, hoping her eyes were playing tricks on her. "Kai, could you come take a look at this, please?"

Kai scrambled out of the cargo area.

"Did you find it?" he asked, thinking of the missing sun stone.

Rania motioned directly in front of them. Now that it was closer she thought that the shape in the water looked like a sea serpent; long and undulating, cutting a dark path through the ice strewn water.

Kai peered through the gloom. "It looks like it's heading to the right of us. If we stay here we shouldn't intersect."

Rania heard a slight tremble in Kai's voice. She knew he wasn't a strong swimmer. If they were capsized she would be able to survive in the water, but would he?

"The ice here is strong enough to hold you," she said, "if it gets close, I'll throw you over to that big flat chunk then come back for you once I get the boat stabilized."

Kai said nothing. They both seemed to be holding their breath.

"If," Kai whispered, "our friend here turns out to be more trouble than anticipated...."

"You mean, if it eats us?" Rania supplied.

"Um, yes. If it decides we look too delicious to pass up, I want you to know... to know...."

"Yes," Rania whispered after a very long pause, "to know what?"

But Kai wasn't listening. All his attention was focused on the monster. Something wasn't quite right.

He barked out a laugh that was startling in the quiet gloom.

"It's not an enormous creature; it's many rather large creatures."

Rania didn't think this was much better. In fact, she thought it might be worse. She stared at the moving mass, trying to see what Kai was seeing. Light reflected off of a long, twisted shape.

"They're narwhals!" she yelled out in relief.

As if at the sound of her voice, the line of elegant whales shifted course in their direction.

Panic set back in. The whales might not want to eat them, but that didn't mean they wouldn't capsize the boat accidentally.

The giant creatures moved slowly, diving down and resurfacing for air and to break up the ice.

As they passed perilously close to the boat Kai realized that he could read their intent.

"They're headed for the open corridor we created in the ice. They were in an enormous fjord, but when the fog rolled in, they knew it was time to head back out to sea."

"But that means," Rania said, "that we can follow the path they left through the ice back to the island. We don't need the sunstone- we have a trail."

The boat jostled as the whales swam by. Rania fought the urge to dive in and swim with them in the quiet fog. She longed to know what their seemingly choreographed progression looked like from under the water. She would never forget the wonder of watching them disappear into the fog.

She and Kai sat there watching long after the last in line was gone.

Rania finally broke the silence. "What were you going to tell me," she asked, "when you thought we were goners?"

"What do you mean?" Kai asked, shifting back to his navigating spot.

"You said you wanted me to know something."

"We better get a move on, or our path is going to close back up," he said evasively.

Rania put her hands in the water and started moving the currents to get the boat back in motion.

"It must have been pretty embarrassing if you're working *this* hard to get out of telling me."

"I was just going to say that there must be lemmings in Valhalla, so death won't get in the way of you sampling the most delicious food on earth."

Rania laughed out loud. "Thank Odin for that!"

31

The King of the Mountain

It was a dark and quiet trek up the mountain. Linnea had lost all sense of time when Astrid stopped and handed her a water skin.

"The entrance isn't far off now," she whispered. "I just wish we could obscure our trail a bit. It feels wrong to travel straight towards the portal."

Linnea bit her lip. Since Astrid and her sisters were sharing their secret with her, she decided it was only right to share hers.

"I might be able to help with that."

Astrid put the water skin back in her pack as Linnea closed her eyes and reached out her senses.

It didn't take long for three of the Breezes who had helped her during the tournament to rustle up.

"Princess Astrid, meet the secret of Pahl's success. These are the wind spirits who made it possible for him to collect the golden apple."

It was to Astrid's credit that her mouth only formed a comic 'O' and didn't gape all the way open. After recovering herself, she curtseyed to the Breezes and thanked them profusely.

Linnea turned to them and asked, "Could you hide our trail and maybe send our scent in another direction?"

The Breezes whooshed about them and took a handkerchief from Astrid and a head scarf from Linnea to help in the task.

"Thank you!" Linnea called quietly as they bustled off, wafting leaves and smoothing out boot prints as they went.

When they were out of earshot, Astrid asked, "Are you an enchantress? I had heard that magic runs in your family, but that was simply amazing! I've never seen a corporeal elemental outside of the under-realms, let alone communicated with them."

"No, no," Linnea assured her, "I'm just...," but then she stopped. She didn't know what she was. Rose spawn? A 'gift from nature itself'? She had heard the story of her birth told in that way since she was a child, but what did it even mean?

Thankfully, Astrid didn't seem to need her to finish her sentence. She put a hand on Linnea's shoulder and said, "Whatever you are, I'm glad of it. Your friends will make our escape and the concealment of the Faerie entrance much easier. Thank you."

The foot-hills were hard to navigate at night, especially since the moon kept dipping behind clouds, but Astrid went on without hesitation. The packs of supplies that her sisters had put together seemed to be entirely filled with food. When Linnea showed some concern about not having blankets or a tinder box, Astrid chuckled.

"Don't worry; we've got lots of non-perishables inside the gateway."

Astrid explained that the sisters usually used a portal within the castle when they would visit the Faerie realm, but they soon learned that there were other openings between the worlds, if you knew what to look for.

"Annalisa made it her mission to map out as many portals as we could find. We've got this entrance well provisioned."

"Your sisters are amazing. I can't imagine my sisters working together like yours do."

"But you and your sisters sound so adventurous! You're all going to seek the stones to heal your mother by yourselves. Until now, I've never really done anything without at least two of my sisters tagging along."

Linnea heard a small catch in her friend's voice. "I'm sorry that I've come and messed things up for you. I didn't mean to cause you to have to leave your home."

Astrid laughed, but it sounded brittle in the night air.

"You have made it possible to be with the man I love and to escape my father's tyranny. I am forever in your debt. None of us could save our mothers, but I will do everything I can to help you save yours."

Linnea didn't know how to respond. She knew that the king had been married many times, but she had never really thought about what had happened to his wives.

They walked on in silence until Astrid said, "We're here."

Linnea didn't see anything special about the large moss-covered stone in front of them, but when Astrid put her palm on a bare spot at the base, a door opened in the earth.

"Quickly, come inside," she said. "I'll light the lamps once the door is safely sealed behind us."

Linnea looked at the long, dark staircase leading deep underground and shuddered.

Before Astrid could shut the portal behind them, a small dark shape flew past Linnea's face and into the darkness beyond.

"What was that?" Linnea whispered.

Astrid finished sealing the portal and lit two of the twelve lamps, all lined up on a low niche.

"It was probably a bat or one of the hidden folk in avian form. They sometimes get stuck outside and aren't able to transform back without eating food grown in their own lands."

Linnea was shocked. "Is this Faerie, then? I thought it would be more, I don't know, magical?"

Astrid grinned. "This is just a kind of entryway to the Hidden Lands, Faerie, Underland, whatever you like to call it."

Linnea thought her friend sounded awfully glib for such a pronouncement.

"Aren't you afraid of being stuck here forever, being eaten by the Fae or losing your mind?"

Astrid's response was not very comforting. "Those are mostly stories. If you follow the rules, it's pretty safe."

Linnea was about to ask just how safe was 'pretty safe' when Astrid started walking down a wide stone staircase, running her lantern-free hand along the stone wall to their left. Linnea followed her, wondering what lay in the darkness to their right. Cautiously, she stretched her lamp in that direction.

"You might not want to do that," said Astrid, pausing to look back. "The stairs are wide, but the drop-off on that side can make people dizzy. I looked once, and now I stay as far away as I can and try not to think about it as I descend."

Linnea decided to take her friend's advice and trailed her own left hand on the comforting stability of the rock wall.

"We used to dance here every night when we were children," said Astrid. "Well, not *here*, exactly, but in the Underlands. There's an entrance in a cupboard in the royal nursery. All of we sisters used to sleep there until they noticed our dancing slippers were dirty and worn most mornings. Our father went crazy trying to get the secret out of us. He even sent in spies, but Annika was too clever for them."

Linnea smiled. "She seems like she could handle anything."

"She's the glue that holds us all together," said Astrid. "One night, we had a very close call, and Annika knew that it was not just *us* in danger, but all the Fae and the Huldra Folk, as well. She decided that we should let our father *think* he had found our secret, so we let one of his spies see us escape out a little used back stairway into the woods, where we danced about with paper crowns on our heads."

"Did it fool him, your father?" Linnea asked.

"He believed it, but he was angry. Our punishment was to be split apart- each with a separate bedroom. It was sad, but not half as sad as not being able to visit the Under-realms and see our friends here."

"Have you never been back, then?" Linnea asked.

"Oh, yes, in twos and threes every so often, but never all together. Those days are gone, but we *were* able to map out the other entrances. I think we always knew that one of us might need them to escape one day."

Astrid's head drooped, and her descent slowed.

"And you said there is an entrance near the Giant's city?" Linnea asked.

"It comes out in a large palace called the Houses of Learning. The Giants and the Fae had a cordial relationship. We'll be passing under the mountains while Pahl'ly travels above."

Linnea was going to ask how long their trip would take, when they came to a great boulder blocking their way. There, perched on a niche in the wall like the one with lanterns above, stood the blue bird.

"Where have *you* been?" Linnea chided her old traveling companion. "Was that you who slipped in with us up above?" It took a moment for Linnea to realize that Astrid was holding a deep and formal curtsey.

"Do you know the King of the Mountain, then?" Astrid whispered, aghast.

Linnea turned back to the bird. "You're a king?" she spluttered, then recovered. "I apologize for calling Your Highness McFeatherbritches," she said while giving the best curtsey she could manage after a night of dancing followed by a trek through the dark foot-hills and a climb down a long steep stairway.

The bird bowed his head low in appreciation.

Astrid used her hand to trigger the boulder open, and, with one last whoosh past Linnea's head, the blue bird flew away.

"You called the King of the Mountain McFeather Britches?" Astrid asked, trying hard not to laugh.

"Miss Chirperine McFeatherbritches, if I recall correctly," Linnea admitted.

Astrid broke into hysterical laughter.

"What's his *real* name?" Linnea asked. "I've been trying to guess it for ages."

"We just call him the Mountain King or Bjergkonge. No mortal knows his true name."

"Well, at least I'm not the only one," said Linnea.

As they emerged from the tunnel all thoughts of the Mountain King vanished as she beheld the heart-stopping beauty of the Underlands.

Linnea rubbed her eyes, but the scene before her remained the same. A full moon shone down on rolling hills covered in a thick blanket of snow. Trees dotted the landscape, twinkling with a skin of ice, frozen droplets clinging to branches like crystals.

She turned on the spot, trying to take it all in. The opening from which they had come was disappearing as a snow-dusted boulder rolled back into place.

"But..." she stammered, grabbing Astrid's arm. "But... aren't we underground??? And I distinctly remember that the moon was a crescent tonight."

Astrid laughed. "I forgot how disconcerting it is on your first visit. My sisters and I could never figure out if the portals transport you to another place or just into another version of the same space."

The multitude of questions forming in Linnea's head never made it to her mouth since a small voice behind them took this moment to clear its throat and say, "The King of the Mountain sends transport to the Princess Linnea and her friend as a thank you for her assistance in the over-lands."

Linnea and Astrid spun around to see a magnificent sleigh that had not been there a moment before. It was drawn by a deer-like creature whose many branching antlers looked like they would topple him, if not for the ornate harness and bells.
Linnea thought it was the deer who had spoken until she saw a small gnome or tomte in a red conical hat standing atop the animal's head.
He bowed to the ladies and motioned to the conveyance behind him.

They curtseyed in return, Linnea following Astrid's lead. If their survival depended on knowing the rules of this place then Linnea was determined to not take a step without Astrid's approval.

Astrid didn't seem at all concerned about accepting the gift, so the ladies climbed up onto the sleigh.

It was made of a heavily lacquered, nearly black, wood with inlaid silver scroll-work and symbols.

The bench seat was padded with black velvet cushions, and a thick blanket of the same fabric lay ready for them to pull onto their laps.

When they were settled in comfortably the gnome asked, "To the giant city of Kaempeby?"

Astrid nodded at Linnea, so she replied with a "Yes, please."

Soundlessly, the sleigh glided over the snow, the full moon illuminating their way with a cool glow. Linnea gazed in wonder as the trees flashed by. Soon, they were driving beside a river of ice that snaked through the landscape like a ribbon.

"Where are all the folk?" Linnea asked. "I had always supposed Faerie to be full of magical beings."

"They are shy of strangers, even in their own lands," Astrid explained.

The movement of the sleigh soothed Linnea's exhausted nerves, and soon she was fighting to stay awake.

"You sleep," Astrid told her. "The air here invigorates me. I'll keep an eye on things."

Linnea wasn't sure what Astrid could do if they started going in the wrong direction or were suddenly set upon by wolves, but she was so tired she wasn't sure she even cared. Burrowing down into the covers, she curled her legs up beside her on the bench and fell fast asleep.

It felt like a mere moment later when Astrid was shaking her shoulder gently.

"We're here," she said. "The portal is just beyond the tallest pine."

"How long was I asleep?" Linnea asked as they clambered out of the sleigh.

"The rest of the night," Linnea replied. "It should be morning soon."

Once back on the ground, they each gave a curtsey to the deer and gnome.

"Please give our humblest thanks to the Mountain King," Linnea said. "This has been the finest mode of transport I have ever experienced."

Both the gnome and deer bowed in return and then drove in a smooth arc through the snow to head back the way they had come.

"Well," said Astrid, "your fine gift has put us here *well* before Pahl. I wouldn't be surprised if we didn't see him for another day or two."

"Does he know about your trips to, what did you call it, the Underlands?" Linnea asked.

"Oh, no. We guard our secret well, even from those we love, but once we are married I plan to tell him everything."

Linnea followed Astrid to a boulder that was more like a small hill.

"This is the biggest of the portals," Astrid explained, "for obvious reasons."

It took her a while to find where to put her hand, but soon, the stone rolled away, revealing an ornately carved stone archway.

The palace beyond seemed to be carved entirely from bedrock.

Linnea felt like a doll walking beneath the stone arch. A shiver ran down her spine as she heard the rock grind back into place, cutting off the moonlit snows of Faerie.

As with the other portals, there was a niche in the wall for lanterns, and soon Astrid had one glowing.

"It's just ahead," she said, steering them through the enormous deserted halls.

The sun was just rising as they emerged onto an enormous balcony. A cool Breeze rustled in

Linnea's hair. She sighed and smiled until a booming voice made her nearly jump out of her skin.

"What took you so long?!?"

32

The Princess who Remained

Sylvi awoke in the tower room and smiled at the sight before her. The fireplace blazed cheerfully, illuminating a tray on the side table laden with a delectable-smelling breakfast. Boots was clearly a master of stealth along with all of his other skills.

She reached for a pastry, her smile widening as she noticed that Boots had also laid out two sets of clean clothes for her. One pile held what looked like a page uniform of simple breeches, a tunic and a floppy hat. The other pile was a mountain of light colored underthings and a brocade over-dress, topped with an elaborate headdress.

She smirked as she put on the page boy's clothing, setting the hat at a jaunty angle before heading downstairs.

Boots had been busy marking arrows on the walls in charcoal. "No more getting lost for you!" he told Sylvi when she found him. "I thought you could keep searching for clues in the library while I do my morning chores," he continued. "I'll come find you when it's time for lunch."

Sylvi could find no fault in this plan and happily followed the arrows marked 'library' to begin digging.

She was surprised when Boots came in with a tray what seemed like mere moments later.

"Any luck?" he asked, setting the food on a table.

"I've been looking through this section, but nothing seems to be organized," she sighed.

"Hmmm," said Boots, "maybe we should eat some lunch, and then what do you say to setting aside our academic pursuits for a good old-fashioned treasure hunt? There are plenty of places we haven't checked yet."

Despite their enthusiasm, they didn't find anything that day or the next, and as the days rolled by, they fell into a pattern.

Sylvi spent her time exploring, sorting books and helping Boots with the chores.

As she walked along the now familiar hall to the library, she wondered how her sisters were doing. Were they safe? Had they found their stones already? She pushed aside the thought that time was running out- that she would be the one to let everyone down.

She closed her eyes, took a deep breath and knocked over a small table covered in books. As she bent to pick them up, she noticed that a drawer had jostled open. The journal inside was worn and ink-stained. Sylvi gingerly removed it, brought it over to her favorite nook and began to read.

"Find anything interesting?" Boots asked, coming in a half hour later with the lunch tray.

"Not about any new hiding places to check, but I'm beginning to think that the people of this castle left because of something in the forest and not the troll," she said, catching the roll Boots tossed to her.

"Don't let *him* hear you say that," Boots replied, buttering the next roll for himself. "To hear the

Troll tell it, he single-handedly squished half of the courtiers, and the other half ran away in mortal terror. I created an epic story-song all about it, based on his firsthand account. Please don't tell me I need to make revisions."

Sylvi laughed. "Well, I think you can leave in the part about them running away in mortal terror. I found this journal. It was written by the king and queen's only daughter. She seems to have been living here by herself after the mass exodus, but there's no mention of a troll."

Boots nudged into the nook beside her to take a look.

"Do you think she's the princess the troll traded for the stone?"

"Maybe," Sylvi said, turning back a page. "Read this part."

"I'm starting to lose hope that I can do this on my own. The forest is closing in. I've sent out the letters; I only pray they make it through and are answered in time." Boots read aloud. "Who were the letters to?"

"I don't know. She didn't write it down, or at least not in this volume. Maybe there's a journal that comes before this one."

"You keep reading," Boots said, jumping up. "I'll search for the lost journal of the princess who remained."

"I like that," said Sylvi. "'The Princess Who Remained'- she needs an epic tale."

"I can sing it for the Troll at dinner and see how he reacts. He keeps giving me maddening hints about stones and hiding places. I'd love to taunt *him* with something. "

Sylvi snuggled back into the nook and started reading. The next section was an inventory of what food remained and a list of ideas for getting more. She could feel the princess's fear and impatience as she waited for her letters to be answered, and then they were.

"No," Sylvi breathed.

"Something good?" Boots called from across the library.

"You'll never guess," she said with a twinkle in her eye. "Your troll is a phony!"

Boots scrambled down the ladder and hurried to Sylvi's side.

"Tell me more," he said curling up next to her.

"It seems," she said, "that your vicious Troll was actually a friend of the prince."

"The prince who supposedly traded the Troll the Gem of Embodiment in exchange for a princess?"

"The very one," she affirmed.

"Wait one moment," Boots said as he jumped out of the nook and rushed away.

Sylvi thought he was off grabbing a book or something else of relevance, but when he came back he was carrying an armful of pillows and a large quilted blanket.

In explanation he remarked, "This is going to be a *really* good story. I thought we should get comfy."

He made Sylvi climb out of the window seat as he added the pillows and arranged them to his liking. Once he was done, they climbed back up, and he put the quilt over them both.

"Now we're ready," he said as he nestled himself into the pillows and closed his eyes. "M'Lady, please begin."

Sylvi had thought she would just tell Boots the facts, but his fanfare made her want to breathe life into the tale.

"Once, there was a mighty forest kingdom that lived in peace and prosperity. The folk believed that they owed their good fortune to a magical gem that had resided in their ancestral castle since the first stone was laid. The king and queen, and therefore the court, however, believed their prosperity to come from generations of wise rule. They had even started work on a new city to the north of the forest with an enormous new castle. Most thought this a grand idea, but the King and Queen's daughter protested. 'The heart of the kingdom is here, with our forest, our gem and these ancient walls that have been good to us.'"

"The Queen and King, and therefore the court," Sylvi went on, "laughed her protests off as the romantic imaginings of a silly girl. Soon after, a messenger came from their kin in the southwest. A horrible plague was ravaging their land, and they requested the use of the Gem of Embodiment to aid them in a mad attempt to heal their people and their king. Most of the royal family chuckled at their naiveté and were all for simply *giving* them the stone, but the princess insisted that the stone be returned. Though the court smiled indulgently, there was a young man in the entourage of the messenger who saw the earnestness in the princess's eyes and vowed inwardly to bring her the stone himself."

Sylvi knew she was taking some liberties with her interpretation of the facts, but it was hard to resist embellishing with such an attentive listener.

"As it would happen," she went on, "He would get his chance."

Boots' hand shot out and grasped her arm.

"Was it the prince?" he gasped, eyes wide open now.

Sylvi was about to say, "yes, my great, great uncle," before remembering that she hadn't told Boots she was related to the royal family that had borrowed the stone. She was about to come clean when he went on.

"So, was she right? Did losing the stone cause problems?"

"Not at first," Sylvi said, "but as the months went on, strange things started happening. People just wrote it off as bad luck, but the princess knew the truth."

Sylvi could practically see the wheels moving in Boots' mind as he started breaking down the story into his next epic poem. Then his eyes came back into focus.

"But I interrupted your story. I'm no better than your horrible sisters."

Syvi laughed. "I don't think they ever interrupted me because they were excited about what I was telling them, so I'll let you off with a warning this time."

Boots settled back in and closed his eyes. 'Please continue. I promise to let you finish without any more outbursts."

"I'm holding you to that," said Sylvi with a smirk before picking back up her narrative.

"When the odd occurrences became too frequent to ignore, the king and queen, blaming the forest and not the loss of the stone, decided to move their court to the new castle earlier than originally intended. The princess refused to leave, and in the end, her family deserted her. For a while, a few loyal friends and servants remained with her at the old castle, but it didn't take long for the 'haunted forest' to scare them off, as well. Desperate and alone, the princess sent a letter with a traveling minstrel, not to her family, but to the kingdom that had promised to return the gem. She hoped to all the gods that the letter would get to them and that they would send someone with the stone before it was too late. It was a long and lonely time, but finally, one morning, her prayers were answered; A prince of Fullanda and his mighty Troll companion appeared on her doorstep bearing the Gem of Embodiment. They returned it to the heart of the castle, but it would take time for the magics of the land and forest to heal. The troll vowed to stay in the castle and keep the gem safe while the prince brought the princess back to her family in hopes that they might one day return."

33

Really, Really Cold Water

Following the narwhal trail was easy, even in the dense fog. It was a river of black surrounded by a world of grays.

"We need to be careful," Rania said. "If the whales came from a fjord, we'll have to change course as soon as we get to the coast. There's no way we could make it up those icy cliffs."

Kai nodded and scanned the fog for any sign of land.

They traveled on through the night, not wanting the trail to freeze up on them. Kai blinked furiously, trying to discern if the hazy darkness to the left was the island or his eyes playing tricks on him.

"L...land- it's land," he croaked out.

"That's great," Rania sighed, "but how do we get to it?"

Kai's laugh sounded more like a groan. An expanse of unbroken ice lay between them and the island.

Rania tested the ice with the spear. It ricocheted off the glassy surface and slid out of reach.

"I'll go get it," Kai said, knowing the ice would hold his weight if it hadn't cracked with Rania's blow.

The ice was covered with a thin layer of snow that made its surface deceptively slippery. Even treading carefully, his front legs shot out from under him, and he slid to the pole in a most undignified manner- rear end pointing to the sky.

Rania's bark of a laugh rang out in the fog-muffled night.

"Sorry," she said, still laughing unrepentantly. "Are you ok?"

"Just bruised my chin... and my dignity," he said, carefully getting his front legs back under him.

"How firm is the ice?" Rania asked.
Kai maneuvered to the other side of the spear, slipping but keeping his feet under him.

"It's not cracking or making any noise at all. How thick is it at the edge?"

Rania looked at the edge of the ice where the boat was resting against it. "About a quarter hands-breath. There's no way we're getting through that, and I have no idea how to get the boat up at this angle. Get back in. We'll see if it's any better near the mouth of the fjord."

Kai retrieved the spear, nosing it back to Rania and then jumped in the boat.

The ice didn't get any thinner as they neared the looming cliff walls of the fjord, and their trail was closing in, making it harder to break through the fine layer of ice that was beginning to form on its surface.

"This is as far as we can go," Rania said, biting her lip, "and I still can't see a way to get the cursed boat onto the ice."

When purchasing supplies for Rania's trip, the selkies had found skis that were made to attach to a small boat. Rania had counted on being able to use the boat as a sled once they hit land, but they would have to use packs if they couldn't get the boat out of the water.

"Maybe I can pull it out if we empty it," Rania suggested.

They carefully climbed onto the ice and then removed the tarp that had been covering their gear. After laying it out flat, Rania began handing parcels out to Kai, who dragged or pushed them into the middle of the tarp. If Rania wasn't able to pull the boat up, she hoped that it might be easier to pull their gear across the ice instead of carrying it.

When the boat was finally empty, Rania tried to pull it up, but no matter what angle she tried, it stayed stubbornly in the water.

Trying hard not to think of how much gear they would need to leave behind once they hit land, they began to pull the load towards the island. It took a while to get the heavy canvas moving, but once in motion, it was relatively easy to keep it moving (with only minimal bruising of dignities).

As the boat started to fade in the fog, Rania stopped.

"I have an idea," she said and started taking off her jacket.

"Um," said Kai, "whatever it is, I'm pretty sure that it's not a *good* idea."

"Don't worry. I've got the selkie goo on me, so I won't feel the cold, and I don't want my clothes to get wet.

Kai turned his back as she stripped down to her under-things.

"Wish me luck," she said as she picked up the boat skis, jostling them in her arms before finding a good balance.

"Good luck?" Kai said as he watched her walk back to the boat.

She dropped the skis a ways from the edge and approached the water. The boat was already held firm in a thin layer of ice that now covered the entire narwhal trail.

Rania couldn't feel the cold, but she didn't know how long the selkie salve would last.

She sat on the edge of the ice shelf and cracked the thin layer holding the boat with her foot. The water looked black and fathomless. Before she could talk herself out of it, she slid in.

Everything was quiet and still in the near-frozen waters. It was eerie, but something in Rania wished to explore the ocean below the ice.

Instead, she closed her eyes and tried to sense if any Nixies lived in the frozen darkness.

She was surprised at how quickly they came, curious about this warm-bodied visitor to their realm.

The water churned as they kicked in unison, lifting the boat to the ice above.

When Rania turned in the water to thank the Nixies for their help, they were already disappearing under the frozen sheet. Silently, one looked back over her shoulder, inviting Rania to join them.

Rania swam forward, trying to see where they were headed, when a splash from behind startled her.

A ball of white fur with four stubby legs seemed to be fighting with the water. Rania's laugh sent out a large bubble of air that got trapped under the ice-sheet. She swam over to Kai and helped him get back up on solid footing.

She was still chuckling as she joined him. "You really can't swim, can you? Did you fall in?"

He shook himself out, sending a cascade of water droplets flying through the air. "I was worried about you. You were under for a long time, and when I saw movement under the ice I panicked."

"I don't need to breathe when I'm under water," she reminded him. She left it at that, not wanting to admit that she had started following the Nixies. A shiver ran down her spine.

Kai misinterpreted the movement. "Let's get you back into your dry clothes."

The walk back to the gear was miserable, the wet ice tried to freeze their feet in place, and Raina was sure she had lost a layer or two of skin by the time she put on her socks. Her undergarments had started freezing stiff and were hard to take off before getting back into her dry clothes.

She cursed at her icicle laden hair, trying to get it all under her large fleece-lined cap.

"These boat skis had better be worth the effort," she mumbled as they trudged back to the boat.

Kai learned many more Fullandan curse words as Rania wrestled the skis into place. He was happy to be useful as a bracing weight - holding things in place by lying on them.

When the job was complete, they were both bruised and exhausted.

Rania slumped onto the ice and rolled to her back with a groan.

"I live on this ice now. You'll have to go fetch me lemmings and force-feed me until a white Bear finds me and makes me his lunch."

Kai slumped down beside her.

"You had to bring up food. Now I'm starving."

Rania turned her head towards their supplies.

"Uhhh. Too far," she whimpered.

They lay there in the cold, silent fog, listening to each other breathe. Then Rania said the one thing she knew would get Kai moving.

"But seriously, what were you so desperate to tell me back on the boat?"

Kai jumped up, flicking Rania in the face with his tail.

"I guess those supplies aren't going to pack themselves," he said. "Get up you lazy devil. I'm not pushing this thing by myself."

Rania rolled to her knees and stood up carefully. Every muscle still ached.

The selkies had explained that once the skis were on the boat it could be pushed easily through the snow, but Rania found it hard to get any leverage on the ice.

"We have got to find a better way of moving this thing," she growled in frustration after falling for the fourth time.

"We're almost back to the supplies," Kai said.

"Yeah, but there's a lot of ice after that. We're going to have to follow the shoreline until we can find a less rocky landing. I wish it hadn't been so calm when this ice froze. If it had been windy, we'd have some texture to push against."

"Why don't you just make waves, like you do in the water?" Kai asked.

"Because this isn't water."

She had started the sentence with a tone of derision, but as she reached its end, a thought emerged.

"Except it *is* water- really, really cold water."

Slowly, she took off one thick mitten and put her hand on the ice. It tingled on her fingers, as if it was listening.

Manipulating water came easily, but this felt different- foreign. She thought of Sylvi and how she talked to living things.

"What would Sylvi say?" she mumbled. "Dear ice, though you have repeatedly tripped me and given me many bruises, I do not hold that against you. Could you please help us now by giving us a textured path by which we might guide our conveyance to shore?"

Nothing happened.

"Is that what your sister really sounds like?" Kai asked.

"Like what?"

"Both flowery and sarcastic at the same time."

Rania laughed. "No, she's actually very respectful and genuine. Guess I don't have much practice at those things, but sarcasm- that I can do in my sleep."

Kai cocked his head. "You're respectful and genuine all the time, but in your own way. Maybe try that."

Rania found it generous of Kai to believe she had it in her, so she gave it a try, not harboring much hope that it would do any good.

Taking a deep breath, she thought about what ice looked and felt like when it froze in turbulent weather- the crunch of it under her feet and the joy of being able to run on the lake near her childhood castle without slipping. She then pictured the path to the supplies with a thin strip of textured ice, just enough to give her feet purchase and small enough that the skis would remain on the smooth ice.

When she opened her eyes a rippling trail lay before them, just as she had envisioned.

34

Windy Revelations

Linnea spun around to see the North Wind hovering on the other end of the balcony.

"What do you mean, 'what took you so long'?" she shot back at him.

But he had already turned his attention to Astrid.

"Your betrothed has been delayed," he told her. "No, don't worry, he is quite safe, but I have sent him on to the coast. I thought it best you leave the southern continent altogether. If you are not afraid to travel by air, I have some Gales that will blow you to him."

"Thank you, Grand Sir," she said with a curtsey and turned to Linnea.

"Will you be alright?" she asked, eyebrows knit in concern.

"I'll be fine," Linnea said, glaring at the North Wind. She turned to her friend and added, "Be safe and greet Pahl and Bert for me."

"I will," said her friend, her eyes glassy as she hugged Linnea goodbye.

"Where will you go? I'll find you when my quest is over."

"I really have no idea," Astrid said with a little shrug, "but I'll write you in Fullanda when we're settled."

"Fullanda!" Linnea gasped, "You *must* go there. My Grandmother will protect you."

"Are you sure?" Astrid asked. "I don't want to impose."

"Fullanda it is, then," said the North Wind, cutting them off. At a flick of his hand, the Gales swept Astrid off her feet and away from the abandoned city.

The North Wind was looking rather pleased with himself when Linnea rounded on him.

"I was going to send a message to my grandparents. You couldn't have waited two more minutes?"

The North Wind did not look apologetic.

"If you hadn't taken so long to get here, I wouldn't be in such a hurry."

"What does that even mean?" Linnea asked. "You know, never mind. I don't want to know. I just need you to bring me Jotunheim." With some reluctance, she added, "Please."

"The stone isn't there," The North Wind said, crossing his arms.

"What? You know about the stones? How do you know it's not there?" she spluttered.

"Because I've looked," he said.

"You've looked? Everywhere? In the *entire* realm?" she asked, one eyebrow rising ever so slightly.

"Yes," he replied simply, "in *all* the realms."

Linnea stomped her foot. "I don't care if *you've* looked. I haven't. My great, great uncle disappeared with the giants when they were banished. He must have gone with them. I am going to Jotunheim, and if you won't take me, I will just have to find another way."

"There is no other way," the master of winds scoffed, "and you are running out of time."

Linnea glared at him. "You think I don't know that? And what business is this of yours anyway?"

He glared right back at her. "You think you're the only one who cares about your mother? I've spent *years* speeding your grandfather along his way- looking for a wise woman, looking for the stones, looking for a cure! I've scoured every inch of the nine realms myself, searching out clues and tracking down hints. I've set you and your sisters on your paths, finding you help along the way..."

"Wait," Linnea interrupted," you know where the stones are, but you didn't collect them yourself? You set us in harm's way, instead?"

"Knowing where something is and being able to retrieve it are two different things," he replied. "As it turns out, I'm not able to save your mother on my own."

The North Wind's bluster was dying down, but Linnea's flared up.

"What??? You needed us to get the gems, but you didn't think to tell us what was going on? You let me believe that my bad temper got my sisters killed! I was right about you. You *are* an arrogant, self-serving tyrant! All you do is push people around like pawns. Don't you bring all knowledge to the edges of the nine realms? You'd think you might have learned something about communication!"

The North Wind seemed to grow in size. He towered over her.

"You may be my daughter, but nobody talks to me that way!"

"Your what?" Linnea yelled back at him. "I don't know who you think I am, but I am most definitely NOT your daughter."

"Oh, there were days I told your mother I would gladly trade you for that little polite one, Sylvi, but her *elemental* mother would have never made the trade for such an ungrateful, insolent..."

"Ungrateful???" Linnea interrupted. "What am I supposed to be grateful for? And maybe I'd be less insolent if anyone had ever told me I even had a father!"

The North Wind seemed to deflate at her words. "That was your mother's decision," he said. "She knew you would have to live among humans, and she wanted you to feel comfortable there, like you were one of them.

"What are you saying," Linnea asked, all the fight gone out of her. "That I'm not... human?"

35

Library Confessions

"That dirty liar!" Boots said, interrupting Sylvi's story, again. "That devious troll must have been laughing at me the whole time I was composing the epic tale of his great capture of the castle."

"Aren't you just a little bit glad he's not a rampaging murderer?" Sylvi asked.

"Well, truth be told, he always did seem a bit too polite for someone as vicious as he claimed to be. I suppose I shouldn't be too surprised. But wait, if the stone is where it's supposed to be, then shouldn't the land be healed? Wouldn't people want to come back here? You said it yourself; you didn't think the forest was haunted."

Sylvi thought about it. "It didn't seem dangerous, but there was definitely something wrong."

Sylvi nibbled her lip, and then she made a decision. She climbed out of the cozy nest Boots had made for them in the window seat and walked across the library. The cold of the room made her want to crawl back under the blanket.

She turned slowly, looked at him and took a deep breath.

"I have something to tell you," she said.

Boots sat up straight and gave her his full attention.

"I haven't been entirely forthcoming about myself."

Boots nodded as Sylvi went on.

"There is a reason I could feel something odd in the forest. I'm... well, I can do this."

She closed her eyes and made her skin camouflage to match the bookshelves behind her. Then she made it turn to the light shade of green she always preferred at home.

Before she could see Boots' reaction, she rushed on, "and I can communicate with things in nature, including trees."

She put her hand up and waved at a tree out the window. Boots turned in time to see snow falling from the branch of a tree that was waving back at them.

"And," Sylvi continued, "I feel horrible that I haven't said anything, but I didn't know how you would react and... and...."

Sylvi wasn't able to finish her sentence. Hot tears filled her eyes and spilled over just as Boots folded his arms around her.

"Never feel," he said, "that you have to hide any of your amazing self from me."

She hiccupped and cried more at the relief.

"Well," she said, biting her lip again. "There is *one* more thing."

Boots brought her a chair and then sat on the floor in front of her.

"Lay it on me. I can take anything. Well, as long as you're not about to tell me that you're a princess," he said with a smirk and a wink.

She knew it was a joke, but her courage gave out.

"I snore," she said. She wasn't even sure if it was true, but it was the first thing that came into her head.

Boots laughed. "You and me both! I could give the Troll a run for his money in the snoring department, if what my old master told me is accurate, but wait," he said, "could you talk to... to... nature and ask if it knows if the gem is hidden outside the castle?"

Sylvi's face fell. "I could, but I'm starting to feel like the stone shouldn't be removed again. We don't know what the repercussions could be. The princess doesn't go into detail about the horrors of the wood when the gem was away, but it must have been terrifying. Even her loyalist companions left her in the end."

"You're right," Boots said, "but we know what will happen if you don't bring the gem to your mother. Don't worry- the Troll and I are here to watch over things while you're away, and from what the journal says, it took quite a while for things to get bad. Besides, would it be so horrible to have to come back here after your quest is complete? You *did* give me exclusive rights to your epic tale, and I'll need to hear all the details of how it ended."

Sylvi's smile was a weak thing, but Boots knew he could strengthen it, given time.

"Besides," he went on, "I'm looking forward to hearing all about the looks on your horrid sisters' faces when you get back before them. "Come on," he said, "we've got work to do!"

Boots bundled her into a warm cloak and dragged her out into the frigid air. The snow had drifted away from this part of the castle, so they were able to walk into the outskirts of the wood.

When Sylvi tried reaching out her thoughts to the spirit of the forest, who had guided her on her journey, only silence greeted her. Then she reached out to the sleepy winter trees around them. They, too, were silent, but she could feel gentle pulses of energy coming from the castle.

"I think it's inside the castle," she told Boots. "Good," he said, rubbing his hands together and stomping, "because it's much warmer in there."

They hurried back inside and warmed themselves by the stove.

"Don't worry," Boots said. "I'll re-double my efforts to get information from the Troll, and we'll keep up the search. We'll find it!"

As they hung their outerwear up on pegs by the kitchen door, Sylvi smiled and gave no thought to the fact that her skin had remained a lovely shade of green.

36

A Message from Above

The newly textured ice made pushing the boat-sled nearly effortless.

Rania pushed as Kai ran alongside.

"You could ride, you know," she told him, "and save your energy."

But Kai insisted that he enjoyed a good trot after being stuck on the boat for so long.

Neither of them said what was really on their minds. They had been jogging along the coast all day and still hadn't found a spot where they could get on land. The cliffs rose and fell to their right but never got low enough to even climb their way up. In the fading light, Kai could see that Rania was slowing down.

"I know you said," he began, "that you didn't want to rest for the night until we were on solid ground, but this ice is as solid as it gets until next spring, and I see a nicely protected spot at the base of the cliffs."

It didn't take long to get the sled in place and crawl under the oiled canvas into their cocoon of sheepskins and woolen blankets.

After the effort of the afternoon, Rania was sweating under her layers of warm clothing.

"Do we have any of the dried herring left?" she asked as Kai nosed into their supplies and dragged out a water skin.

"I never thought I'd get sick of fish," he said, squirming back into one of the supply packs, "but I may never be able to eat herring again after this trip."

Rania munched happily on the salty strip he dragged out for her.

"The end of this trip," she repeated. "What are we going to do at the end of this trip?"

"You mean besides eat fresh food and clean ourselves regularly?"

Rania threw a herring strip at his head, and Kai caught it in his mouth mid-air.

"Are you saying I stink?" she asked.

"Yes," he replied with a foxy grin.

"But seriously," she said, "I've been thinking-when I get the stone and use the ring from my grandfather, I think you should make sure you're touching me when I activate it. Maybe then the magic will transport us *both* back home."

After a pause, she went on.

"I mean, I know you said you would be fine staying on the island for the winter, and then you would use your selkie wish to get to Fullanda once the oceans open up, but maybe we should try to see if you can go with me. You can get just about anywhere from Fullanda, you know, if you decided our small rodents aren't up to your standards."

Kai cleared his throat. "I mean, who can say no to a winter in a palace and food that is not dried herring?"

"You know," Rania said, "If you don't want to come with me, I might try to bring some of the herring instead. This stuff is brilliant." She took another big bite and smiled roguishly at him.

The next day the cliffs gradually lowered until the shore was level with the sea. The sled became harder to push once it was on land, but Rania convinced the snow to flatten out under the skis to smooth their way.

"Does the fog seem to be lifting?" Rania asked as they headed inland. It had been getting thinner over the last day, but now the sun finally seemed to be pushing it completely away.

The selkies had told them to head towards the giant volcanic crater at the center of the island. This was easy during the day since it loomed large in the distance, but with the fog gone, a clear sky would mean they might be able to travel after the sun went down, a mere four hours after rising.

Rania looked back towards the sea to gauge how far they had come. She put her hand up to shield her eyes from the glare of the snow.

"Do you see that?" she asked Kai. "Looks like an eagle or something."

He looked in the direction she pointed.

"Nope. It's a gyrfalcon. Oh, and it just caught something. I bet it was a lemming. I told you they're tasty. Everyone loves lemmings except you."

"A gyrfalcon?" she asked, a lump forming in her throat.

"Yep. Looks like it's heading this way."

"It can't be. It just can't be." She mumbled.

"Don't worry," Kai reassured her, "gyrfalcons don't attack people- that I know of anyway."

"No," she explained, "it's just that my grandfather has a... I mean, there's a gyrfalcon who likes to help my grandfather deliver messages. I know it can't be him, but... what if it is?"

The tension in Rania's jaw was visible as they waited, watching as the bird flew straight towards them.

"Oh, stars," Rania breathed, "he has something attached to his leg."

Kolbein soared over their heads, making a graceful loop before dropping the lemming from his talons and then landing on a rock near Rania.

"Kolbein!" Rania cried, running to him. "It is you, you amazing bird."

The gyrfalcon hopped towards her and held out the leg with the message attached.

Rania's hands shook as she untied it and began to read aloud.

"My dear girls, word just reached me of the shipwreck at the Varm River. I am sending messengers to the locations I suspect the gems to be, in hopes that they will find you and that all is not lost. I beg you to use your rings and come home to us. Do not put yourselves in further danger. Our last hope for finding a magic user with a cure has been in vain, so I am heading home to be with your mother when she wakes. I pray to all the gods that I will see you there. My deepest love, Grandfather."

Her voice cracked and she fell to her knees. When the comforting weight of Kai's furry body leaned against her back she let out a deep breath. She wasn't alone; she had Kai and the knowledge of the Selkie Queen.

"I have to find something to write back with," she said. "They need to know that I'm alive, but I am *not* giving up on this quest."

She jumped into the boat and started rummaging around for a piece of coal, a burned piece of hardtack, anything. Then a thought came to her. She climbed back out of the boat and pulled the knife from her boot.

"What's that for?" Kai asked nervously.

Rania took off her mittens and cut the leather band from her wrist.

"We're nearly there. I don't need my timekeeper anymore. She placed the bracelet on the rock and carved into its surface- 'home soon-R'.

After fastening it to Kolbein's leg, she tried petting him as she remembered Sylvi doing.

Kolbein bumped his head against her affectionately before leaping into the air and flying off.

As Rania watched him disappear across the white expanse, Kai eyed the abandoned lemming. "Think he's coming back for that?"

37

Linnea Borealis

"Am I human?" Linnea repeated.

The North Wind shrank back to near human size. He sat on the bottom step of a stone stairway. Looking Linnea in the eye, he said, "Can humans call the winds, mold the waters or coax the earth?"

Linnea swayed slightly and put a hand out to steady herself against a pillar.

"Well," she said, "no, but... my mother can control fire, and she's human."

The North Wind's brow furrowed slightly. "Yes... a bit- half to be exact."

Linnea took a deep breath and counted to five. After letting it back out she sat on the ground in front of the being that claimed to be her father.

"Please, just tell me. I'm sick to death of pretty stories that just point vaguely to half-truths."

The North Wind smiled. "I prefer plain talk, as well. I'll try to be brief."

It was Linnea's turn to smile. "I don't need you to be brief- just be specific. I always thought that 'pregnancy by flower bud' thing sounded rather suspicious."

"No," he said with a chuckle. "That part is entirely accurate, if not complete."

"Really?" she asked, incredulously. "But why did she want children so badly? She was only nineteen, and why the rose-bud method to get one? Didn't anyone want to marry her?"

"Quite the contrary," he said, leaning forward. "Your mother had *dozens* of suitors, human and otherwise, but she was never the type to show preference or make offence. Or, perhaps, it was just that no one suitor ever caught her particular fancy. Whatever the case," he said, warming to his tale, "she thought that having a child would ensure Fullanda had a queen, and, since human ideas of matrimony can be rather restricting, she decided to have a child the same way her mother did."

"Wait right there," Linnea interrupted. "My mother has a father- my grandfather. You're not saying... wait, what are you saying?"

The North Wind's laugh rustled Linnea's hair. "I'm not saying anything was amiss between your grandparents, simply that they could not conceive a child. When the stones of power weren't returned to the lands that had loaned them, bad luck fell on Fullanda. Towns flooded, crops failed and no one with royal blood was able to conceive a child. Your grandmother, ever a resourceful soul, found a loophole, with the help of a wise woman, of course."

It took a moment to sink in. "So, my grandmother ate rose buds, too?"

"One, to be exact," the North Wind explained. "It was a condition of the magic- that she eat only one."

"But my mother ate all three. She didn't follow the rules."

The North wind gave her a sad smile. "As I've said, your mother never liked showing preference."

Then Linnea finally understood.

"That's why she's dying," she said, "We did this to her."

"No," said the North Wind, a bit more forcefully than intended. "She made her own decision, and she has never regretted it. You are her world. She would tell you it was worth the price, worth any price. In fact, she tells me that regularly."

"You talk to her regularly?" Linnea asked. "Why did she keep this from us? It might have been nice, you know, to have a father. And how does that work, anyway?" she rushed on. "What about Rania and Sylvi? Wait, you said Sylvi has another mother?"

"Oh, yes, and Rania has two other parents," he replied. "Elementals, giants and gods all vied to place a bit of themselves in those rosebuds, but only three would fit in the cup your mother selected."

"Thank the stars!" Linnea interrupted, "Three of us were just about as much as one palace could handle. I'm sorry, please go on. How was it decided?"

The North Wind chuckled. "There was a great contest. I will tell you all about it one day in exacting detail, but the short of it is that I won my place because of my far-reaching knowledge, next was Frigg, goddess of earth and love, and last were the ocean giants, Ran and her husband, Aegir, who loved the idea of having a daughter who could walk on land. They have nine others who roam the waves."

Linnea had been trying to hold her tongue- so grateful to have someone explain these secrets to her, but at this she burst out.

"Do *I* have any half-siblings?"

The North Wind smiled. "No. You are my one and only."

Linnea's cheeks flushed slightly, and she said, under her breath, as she got to her feet, "I think I like that."

She brushed herself off and put her hands on her hips. "Alright, I'm satisfied for now. Why don't we get to work?"

Without a word, the North Wind flew off the balcony and across the giant courtyard. Linnea ran down the enormous stone steps and across the rubble-strewn ground, nearly tripping over the remains of a fallen statue in her attempt to keep up with him.

Thankfully, he hadn't gone far. As she caught her breath, he gestured towards a bed of delicate pink and white bell shaped flowers.

"I tracked the gem here, but I don't know how to get at it."

Linnea gave a surprised chuckle. "It's the twin flower- Linnea Borealis. It's my grandmother's favorite and how I got my name." She knelt down beside the flowers. Something glowed faintly beneath the dirt.

"It's there!" she said, reaching for it, but before her father could warn her, she was thrown back. He helped her to her feet.

"I've tried everything I can think of to break the spell," he said, "but no matter how hard I blow, it won't budge. I thought, perhaps, it might work if we try together."

"Or maybe," she said, and then stopped.

"Yes?" he prompted.

"What if we try the opposite? What if we try gentleness? There is a song about the twinflower that my grandmother would always sing to us when we couldn't get to sleep. It's one her own grandmother used to sing."

"Even if it doesn't break the spell," said the North Wind, "I would love to hear it."

Linnea knelt back down by the flowers and began to sing.

"Little flower small and white – for my dearest heart's delight. See you blushing finest pink – Will it please her, do you think?"

As she sang, the gem began to glow brighter and push its way through the dirt, like a flower trying to find the sun.

"You and your twin together grow – I'll pick you both so she will know - That what I wish is that we too – Are bound together, just like you."

Once it had fully emerged, Linnea put a tentative hand out towards it. No force hindered her as she picked it from the last bit of earth.

"Do you think you could give me a ride home?" she asked, a radiant smile on her face.

"Better yet," he said, beaming back at her, "would you like to learn to fly?"

38

For Forever & a Day

The days flew by at the castle, but clue after clue led to a dead end.

Sylvi pursed her lips, listening for Boots to return to the library.

"Were you able to get anything out of the Troll tonight?" she asked as he shut the door.

"Nothing," Boots said, looking uncharacteristically deflated.

"Not that the other hints he let slip did us any good. He just kept reminding me to get the lingonberry preserves out of the cellar before breakfast."

Sylvi closed her eyes, trying to keep panic at bay.

"Hey there," Boots said gently, taking her hand. "Don't give up hope yet. We still have all night and most of tomorrow to find it."

"But we've looked everywhere," she said.

"Well, actually," Boots said, a new gleam in his eye, "there is *one* place we haven't looked yet. What if he keeps it with him, in a pocket or something? Trouble is it'll be tricky not waking him up as we search. He's deaf as a doornail, but...."

"But," Sylvi cut in, unable to contain her excitement, "I've got the Nacken's water lily!"

She checked the pouch at her waist just to be sure it was still there. As beautiful and untouched as the day it was picked, the red flower's scent was intoxicating.

Boots' face lit up like sunshine.

"You've got the Nacken's water lily! Perfect! You are brilliant, m'lady," he said as he gave her an elaborate curtsey.

"*We* are brilliant," she corrected, bowing regally in return.

"But first, I need to run down to the cellars to grab those lingonberry preserves."

Sylvi raised an eyebrow.

"Hey, don't give me that look," he protested. "With any luck, you'll be off saving your mother by midnight, so there will be no one left to clean my squished corpse off of the carpet when the Troll doesn't get his preserves in the morning."

"That will never do," Sylvi said. "I like that dress far too much to have it pulverized."

Boots smiled. "It is by far my best, and it brings out the color in my eyes."

"Then lead the way, fair princess Gunhilda. This is my first venture into the bowels of the cellar pantry.

"Really?" Boots asked. "Then this will be a treat! We can regale each other with our scariest stories as we go. You can start with the one you didn't finish yesterday, about the naughty girl who poked around in forbidden rooms and was forced to marry a horrid prince. I'll get the lanterns."

"Do you really hate royalty so much?" she asked, a crinkle forming in her brow.

"Yes," said Boots, lighting two lanterns. "Now get on with your story; we're burning moonlight!"

"Very well," she said, taking one of the lanterns from him. "As you recall, the girl had married the young prince, and they were about to start a family. Soon, they had a lovely daughter, but the night after the birth, the woman's godmother came to her and stole the baby, putting a small amount of blood on the woman's mouth."

"Oooh," said Boots, "creepy!"

He scanned the shelves of preserved foods looking for the lingonberries.

Sylvi froze with fear as a hideous Troll's head, mouth wide in what should have been an ear-splitting roar, caught the light of her lantern. It took her a moment to realize that it was carved from the stone of the central pillar. She went over to it and read the inscription beneath it aloud.

"Hid within is heart made stone - But in exchange a princess lone - Must place her hand inside to prove - Or else the gem will fail to move - Her pledge to me must never sway – To stay here for forever and a day."

Boots looked up from his lingonberry search. "That's interesting, but I don't see how it fits in with the story."

"No," said Sylvi trembling in her excitement. "It's the inscription on the wall. This is it, the Gem of Embodiment. It has to be. We found it! Why didn't you tell me about the inscription?"

Boots joined her and stared at the stone head and carved words.

"Because I've never seen it before," he replied.

Sylvi stared at him in disbelief. "But you said you searched down here. That's the reason I never came down."

"Exactly," he said. "It wasn't here any of the countless times I've been in this room, and the carving doesn't exactly look new. It must be under some sort of enchantment."

"Maybe," Sylvi said, "It only appears when someone born female is present."

"That could be," mused Boots, "or on a full moon, or really, just about anything; fascinating."

Sylvi slowly reached out her hand to put it in the stone troll's mouth, but Boots grabbed it back.

"What do you think you're doing?" he asked in horror. "We have no idea what will happen if someone who isn't a princess puts their hand in there.

"But it's the stone," Sylvi protested. "We found it!"

Boots took her by the shoulders and looked her in the eye. "Don't worry, we'll figure out how to get the stone, even if I have to feed every horrid princess in the known realms to the wretched thing. I just don't want to take a chance, especially with you. We've got to find out more. There has to be something about this in the library."

A panic was rising in Sylvi. "But we've spent days searching the library, and nothing like this was mentioned in any of the books. And what if the carving disappears? You said it yourself; we don't know what caused it to show up tonight. It might only appear for ten minutes every hundred years or on every other Thursday. I don't want to miss my chance!"

"Hmmm," said Boots. "How about this- you stay here and make sure it doesn't disappear, with the promise you won't do anything rash while I am away, and I will go up and get supplies- parchment and coal to make a rubbing of the inscription, reference books, chisels, hammers, some food and coffee, lots of coffee. We can stay up all night giving it our best shot. What do you say?"

Sylvi gave a slight nod of her head, and Boots flashed her a radiant smile.

"I'll be right back," he said and turned to leave.

Sylvi didn't hesitate. She pulled the red water lily from her pouch, pursed her lips and blew.

It didn't take long for Boots to feel the effect. He staggered forward. Sylvi rushed to catch him and gently eased his unconscious form to the ground. She rearranged his sleeping body to make him as comfortable as possible on the hard stone floor.

"I'm sorry," she said, moving a stray lock of hair out of his eyes.

Taking a deep breath, she stood up and walked over to the carved troll head.

"I promise to stay here for forever and a day."

Shaking, she placed her hand in the gaping stone mouth palm up.

Her breath hitched as something hard, smooth and heavy fell into it.

A tear of relief ran down her cheek as she pulled her hand out and looked at the prize. She gave herself a moment to appreciate its beauty before taking off her ring and walking back to Boots.

Putting the stone in his pocket, she kissed him on the cheek.

"Say hello to everyone for me," she said as she slipped the ring on his pinkie and turned it three times. When the ring started to glow she released his hand and whispered, "Home."

39

Shedding Skins

That night the sky was perfectly clear. Despite the cold, Rania and Kai had opted to eat their dinner outside. The Aurora danced and rippled across the sky in shades of green, white, pink and purple on a backdrop of countless stars.

"If I had a lifetime supply of selkie-balm to keep me warm," Rania said, "I could get used to living in a place like this."

Kai smiled inwardly, then asked, "Or a fine fur pelt like mine?"

"Ewww," Rania answered, misunderstanding. "I could never wear fox fur now. How horrid."

They watched in silence for a while before Kai tried again. "What if it grew naturally?"

Rania cocked her head to one side, considering. "That would be glorious, but I'd have to be able to take it off for swimming, kind of like the opposite of the selkies. I'd miss the feel of the water on my skin too much."

Kai's mind hummed. 'Glorious'- he could work with that.

The next morning, Rania put on every piece of clothing she could find.

Kai stifled a laugh when he saw her.

"I wish the selkie balm kept me from feeling heat as well as it keeps out the cold. I'm going to be cooked by the time we get there."

"Did the Selkie Queen say why you needed to do this?" Kai asked.

"Sort of. Mostly, I'm just going on blind faith."

They abandoned the sleigh-boat at the base of the crater.

"If I'm not transported with you when you activate the ring, I'll den up in the boat for the rest of the winter. Then I'll ask the selkies for transport to Fullanda in the spring, that is, if you still want me."

"You better get transported with me. How will I stand the rigors of home life after this relaxing vacation with you?"

There was a spring in Kai's step as they began the climb up the steep slope. Thankfully, the lip of the crater came down to meet them as they traveled along the side.

As they ascended, the glacier behind the crater came into view, enormous and riven with blue-green fissures.

"Glad we landed on this side of the island," Kai whispered. "That would have taken forever to cross."

Rania just nodded. Now that they were close to their goal she wished she had read more about the Lindworm and this island in her grandfather's journal. They had been lucky so far, but would it hold?

They scrambled up the last bit of ground as quietly as they could and lay on their bellies, peering over the edge.

The inside of the crater consisted almost entirely of black volcanic rock. It made a stark contrast with the exquisite lake of sparking deep aquamarine at its center and the creature lying on its shore.

It looked like a fine alabaster carving of a serpent with a circlet of gold resting on its majestic forehead. Rania was transfixed by its beauty. Could this really be the monster the Selkie Queen had warned her about?

Kai shuddered beside her. "Those are some serious fangs. Hard to tell from here, but they must be at least as long as your forearm."

Rania shifted her gaze to the lindworm's mouth, and her reverie was broken. The long white fang made an elegant arc down to a murderously sharp point. She turned to Kai to tell him he didn't need to follow her into danger, but the look on his face stopped her words.

The descent was littered with small volcanic pebbles that seemed intent on grabbing their feet out from under them.

When they reached the bottom, after far too many rock slides and curse words, Rania was surprised to see that the serpent still appeared to be sleeping. A hope sparked in her mind- maybe it was dead. They hadn't seen any creatures on the island larger than a lemming. Maybe the king snake had eaten them all long ago and then starved.

She crept quietly closer, not wanting to wake it and prove her hope wrong. The enormity of the wyrm became more apparent as they neared the lake.

As sweat rolled down Rania's back, her mind screamed at her to run while she could, but her feet kept moving her forward.

A sparkle in the lake caught her attention. She peered into the water, thinking to see a fish or maybe a water sprite. Kai shook his head and blinked just as Rania realized that the lake was strewn with gems and jewels and glittering gold coins.

Rania crouched to whisper in Kai's ear.

"Look for a clear stone- long and uncut- about the length of my pinkie finger."

They scanned the lake bed looking for the stone, but there was so much treasure, she didn't know if she could find it even if the Lindworm *was* dead.

"Looking for anything specific," a smooth voice rumbled, "or are you just here to gape?"

Rania nearly yelped but caught herself in time. Gathering what composure she could, she tried to remember the Selkie Queen's instructions.

1. Wear all the clothing you have with you.
2. Be polite.

Rania gave the giant serpent as elegant a curtsy as she could muster. Now was the hard part- remembering all the lines that the Selkie Queen had made her memorize.

"Oh great Prince Lindworm, I am Princess Rania of Fullanda, and I am here to reclaim what is rightfully mine."

The Lindworm looked her over.

"Fullanda, you say? What could I possibly have from so far a kingdom?"

As the serpent spoke, his enormous teeth flashed in the morning sun. Rania thought Kai's estimate had been conservative. They were probably as long as her leg. She tore her eyes away from their sharp points and said, "The Crystal of Cognizance."

The Lindworm narrowed his eyes.

"That *is* a great treasure," he said in his silky grumble of a voice, "and the centerpiece of my collection."

As if by chance, a stone in the exact center of the lake seemed to catch the light and twinkle at them.

Rania gasped. There it was; just like the drawing in her grandfather's journal.

"What can one such as you give me in exchange?" the Lindworm asked.

Rania paused, not really wanting to say what the Selkie Queen had told her she must. After a moment she squared her shoulders and said, "You may have me for your lunch, if you give my friend here the stone."

Rania thought the sound she heard was an avalanche, but soon realized that it was the Lindworm laughing.

"Lunch? You're not much more than an afternoon snack! Besides, how do I know that what is under all of those trappings is even worth the effort? Take off your coat and that ridiculous hat, and we shall see."

"I will remove them if you shed a skin." Rania replied.

"Very well," he said, "It was about time to lose it anyway."

Rania made sure she concentrated on unfastening her buttons, as she had no interest in watching the enormous snake slither out of his outermost skin.

"Now what say you?" she asked once her coat and hat lay in a pile on the ground beside her. "My friend is anxious for his prize."

Kai shifted uncomfortably beside her.

The lindworm tutted. "I'm not convinced. How do I know there's any meat under all that fabric? Take off your over-dress and boots, and then you might look a bit more palatable."

"I could remove them," Rania replied, "but only if you shed another skin."

"Very well, very well," he said.
This skin took him longer to slither out of, but soon they both had shed another layer.

"And now, am I fit for your delicate digestion?" Rania asked.

"No! That is the bulkiest under-dress I have ever seen, and heavens knows what else you've got on under there. You'd give me indigestion for a week.

"The bargain is the same," Rania insisted. "One layer of mine for one layer of yours."

"So be it," the beast said and began scratching his skin against the rock face to remove it.

The Lindworm was raw and pink when he was done. He glared at Rania, shivering convincingly in her woolen stockings and chemise.

"Now you look good enough to eat," he growled.

"May I say goodbye to my friend first?" she asked.

"Don't be long. I'm hungry," he replied.

Rania got on her knees to give Kai a hug.

"I'll turn the ring the second I have the stone and feel your paw on my shoulder."

Kai leaned into the hug but didn't say a word.

As soon as Rania was back on her feet, she ran at the lindworm, taking it by surprise. She knew that the force of her body hitting his wouldn't be enough to knock him into the water, so Rania summoned a mighty wave to drag them both into the depths of the lake.

The Selkie Queen had told her that she must hold on to Lindworm under the water for a count of seven, but the serpent was writhing and thrashing so fiercely she nearly flew off.

As soon as the time was up, she let go and swam to the bottom of the lake.

The fight had knocked the treasure about and kicked up sediment from the lake bed.

Hoping to all the gods that the chaos would make it harder for the lindworm to find her, Rania grabbed at anything that sparkled, tossing away sapphires and diamonds. Suddenly, something sharp hit the back of her hand. She grasped at it, fumbling in the water before it was safely clutched in her hand- the rock that would bring her mother back to them. She clutched it to her and was about to surface to find Kai when she felt a warm touch on her shoulder.

With a sigh of relief, she twisted her ring three times and thought 'home' with all her might. Instantly, the lake disappeared and was replaced by something prickly. She looked about, trying to see where the ring had taken her. It was the hay loft above the horse stables- her favorite hiding spot when playing with her sisters. It had worked! She turned to hug Kai and saw a shirtless man half buried in the hay.

40

Homecomings

Rania flinched back from the man. What was he doing in the hay loft, and why wasn't he wearing any clothing?

He blinked rapidly and rubbed his eyes. Then, seemingly startled by the action, held his hands out and examined them.

"K... Kai?" Rania stammered. The man looked around and then back at her, brow furrowed.

"Who's Kai, and where are we?" he said slowly.

Rania backed towards the ladder, stone still grasped in her hand.

"We're in Fullanda- in the castle stables." The horses shifted nervously in their stalls below as if to confirm her statement.

"I'm home?" the man gasped.

Rania wanted to ask more questions, but she found this man unsettling.

He shivered violently and burrowed into the hay.

"I'll get you something to wear and a blanket," Rania said, sliding down the ladder.

She was still soaking wet, but the selkie balm hadn't worn off yet. Her mind raced as she searched for warm things.

The man's hair was also wet. Had she transported him instead of Kai? Or was he Kai back in his human form? He seemed to be of middle years. How old *was* Kai? Do enchantments change how people age? But, wait, the man said he was home when she told him they were in Fullanda. Kai wasn't from Fullanda, was he?"

She found a stack of horse blankets and an old pair of boots. It would have to do to get him into the castle.

She climbed, one armed, back up the ladder-ready to get some questions answered.

The man took the blankets gratefully, and Rania turned her back so he could wrap himself up in relative privacy.

"We're not far from the castle," she said. "Once we're there, I can get you more appropriate things to wear, and you can warm up by a fire."

"The castle?" he said in wonder. "Then I really am home. How... how has this happened?"

"Who are you?" Rania blurted out, not answering his question.

"I'm... not sure."

Rania shivered and wondered how long the selkie balm would last. "We'll be more comfortable inside. Do you feel up to walking?"

They scrambled down the ladder. The horses were now thoroughly unsettled. Rania tried to calm them, wondering why she hadn't seen any grooms or stable boys. She grabbed a blanket for herself before opening the stable door. She had always thought it a quick jaunt to the side entrance of the castle, but the gusting winds blew snow across their path, making even a 'quick jaunt' dangerous.

They went as rapidly as they could, but it was slow going. The man shivered badly under his thin blankets and stumbled as she tried to get him to move faster.

Rania cursed as an icy wind pushed at their backs, and then she heard her name. Whirling around, she saw her sister coming to ground with the North Wind at her side.

"Linnea," she croaked out, tears prickling in her eyes. Her sister ran to her and wrapped her in a warm embrace.

When her eyelashes threatened to freeze together, Rania pulled away. "Let's get inside," she said. "I want to hear all about your journey. Did you *fly* here???"

When they got to the door, Rania and the man in blankets rushed inside, but Linnea paused. The North Wind stood looking uncertain several paces back.

"What's taking you so long?" she asked, opening the door wide for him to enter.

A smile lit up his face as they went inside, arm in arm.

41

Awakening Lost Memories

Linnea smiled as she walked down the familiar hallway with her father.

They almost ran into Rania and her strange companion as they came out into the grand hall.

Rania pointed to a disturbance directly across from them. The guards were arguing with a young woman in an elaborate yet antiquated dress.

The woman's voice was low and rough as she tried to pull free of the two guards that held her arms.

"As I said before, I have no idea how I woke up on the floor of your library or, indeed, how I even came to be in this castle."

"The library! If she hurt Mother...." Rania said, rushing towards the guards, Linnea close on her heels.

"Princesses, you're back," a guard gasped, open mouthed. "Alert their majesties at once," he told one of his compatriots, who saluted and ran off.

"Has our mother been harmed?" Rania asked, turning the prisoner around to get a look at her. It took Rania a moment to register that the woman was actually a young man.

"Your Majesties," the prisoner said with a curtsey, "assuming that your mother is the woman asleep in the room yonder, I did her no harm. I merely *looked* at her after I woke on the floor next to her couch. I am not sure what devilry has brought me here, but I am in desperate need of getting back to my own castle, so if you would inform these men to kindly release me, I will be on my way."

The guards held their prisoner firm.

"Is it true?" Rania asked the head guard. "Is our mother unharmed?"

"And is Sylvi back yet?" Linnea added.

The prisoner's eyes widened to the size of saucers.

"Sylvi? Your mother is in... an enchanted sleep. Horrible sisters, you're the horrible sisters! Oh heavens, she's a princess, and I am an ass."

They all stared at the stranger, trying to make sense of his babbling.

He stopped talking, closed his eyes, took a deep breath, and said, "Sylvi is in the cellar of a castle at the northern end of the Westerback forest. I am guessing," he said, digging in his pockets," that she traded herself for a stone and has sent me, her humble servant Boots, to deliver it." He held out his hand and opened it to reveal a blood-red gem. "Although, she could have just *asked*," he mumbled under his breath.

Before anyone could properly take in the meaning of his words, the Queen and King rushed into the hall.

"Girls!" their grandmother cried out, falling to her knees on the hard stone floor.

Rania and Linnea rushed to her, and soon felt the strong, loving arms of their grandfather encircle them all.

"Mother?" said the man in blankets staggering towards them. He rubbed his eyes as the queen looked up at him.

The man furrowed his brow. "You, you have her hair and her crown, but...," he squinted at her, not knowing how to end his sentence.

"Uncle... Axel?" the queen asked, disbelieving. "But it can't be. Are you his great grandson? He disappeared returning the Crystal of Cognizance years ago."

"How many years? How long have I been gone?" he asked, his legs giving out on him.

"Nearly seventy years have passed. My grandmother kept a miniature portrait of her lost brothers with her at all times. I remember staring at it when I would sit on her lap. She didn't want them... you to be forgotten. Where have you been all this time?"

The man shook his head. "I was traveling on my way to return the stone," he said haltingly. "The ice came in early and trapped our ship. A small party set out in search of a settlement or any kind of sustenance. A blizzard came up out of nowhere, and I was separated. When it cleared, I was at the edge of a giant crater, looking down on a sparkling blue lake. In my thirst, I stumbled down the crater walls and found that the lake was full of sparkling treasure."

He shuddered before continuing. "It... lit a fire in me. I tried to gather it up, all of it, but grew exhausted with the effort. I lay down to sleep near the bones of an enormous serpent, and when I woke I had no desire to leave."

"You were the lindworm!" Rania gasped. "The treasure must have had an enchantment on it. Is that what the cryptic selkie instructions about 'sloughing skins' was all about- breaking the spell? But if you're the lindworm, then that means that Kai...." She couldn't finish her sentence. She had left him behind. It struck her like a blow.

Linnea took her sister's hand. "Who's Kai?" she asked gently.

"Someone who helped me find this," she said as she opened her hand to reveal the crystal she had retrieved from the lake.

"Then we have them all," said Linnea, producing the Soul Stone.

"Them *all*?" said their grandfather. "Does that mean my little Sylvi is here, too? Where is she?"

Linnea walked over to Boots and guided him to her grandparents.

He curtseyed gravely to the king and queen.

"Your granddaughter is cunning, kind and brave, but I beg your leave to return to her as quickly as may be accomplished. She has no fear, and I worry that the castle troll is not entirely safe, and I never explained to her how he likes his coffee and if he hurts *one* hair on her head...."

The King held up a hand for silence.

"Do you believe that our Sylvi is in immediate danger?"

"No," Boots admitted.

"Then you must delay your journey long enough to see her mother awakened. Sylvi will want to know that the people she loves are *all* safe and that her sacrifice was not in vain."

42

Curse or Consequence

At the suggestion of waking her daughter, Queen Christina rose to her feet, wiped her eyes, and squared her shoulders.

In a moment, Uncle Axel had been sent off for a bath and clothing, and Boots had been released from the guards. That done, she motioned those remaining to follow her to the library.

"Family only," she said to Edvard as he opened the door for her. "This one," she said, indicating Boots, "is standing in for Sylvi."

The guard shifted uncomfortably when the North Wind neared the door.

"This one," Linnea said, mimicking her grandmother, "is family." And with that, she put her arm through her father's and drew him into the library.

They all gathered around Elin's sleeping form. "How does it work?" Rania asked, fidgeting with her stone.

"It's hard to know for sure," the King answered. "None of my research mentions the specifics of the construction. Rania, why don't you place your stone first?"

"You want *me* to put the stone in the crown?" she asked nervously.

They didn't answer but merely watched her expectantly, so she walked forward.

Her mother looked serene. Rania kissed her gently on the cheek and fit her stone into the perfectly formed shape on the crown. It pulsed with light as it clicked into place.

"Linnea, you go next," the Queen said.

The North Wind knelt at Elin's side and took her hand into his as Linnea leaned over and put their stone into place. It too began to glow.

Boots tried to hand his stone to the King.

"No, you have earned the right to do this thing for Sylvi," he said.

Boots bowed his head before fitting the final stone into place.

The moment it connected, the entire crown began to glow.

"How long do you think it takes?" Rania asked Linnea under her breath.

The crown continued to glow, but Elin didn't move.

Quite suddenly, a fire roared to life in the fireplace, startling them all in the quiet of the moment.

Everyone flinched back as a living flame emerged from the blaze and ran towards the sleeping princess. Stunned faces gasped as it gathered her in its arms and danced her around the room.

It had been such a long time since Elin's Fire Imp familiar had burned so brightly. Her daughters didn't even recognize it, but the Breezes, Nixies and Nymphs of Fullanda Castle heard its joyful call and were soon filling the library with their wild dancing and song.

The humans and the lord of the winds stood back and marveled at their revels.

In the midst of the chaos and joy, Elin awoke. Her Fire Imp put her down and soon she was laughing and dancing along with the elementals in robust abandon.

When she caught sight of the shocked faces of her family she laughed and ran to them, hugging them all in turn.

"But where is my Sylvi?" she asked, trying to find her in the crowd. "This is a marvelous dream, but I can't believe my mind would conjure you all for me and forget one of my dear daughters."

"Sylvi is fine, Mother," Linnea said, taking her hand. "She couldn't make it just yet, but she sent a friend in her place."

Linnea lead her mother over to Boots, who was looking on in wonder from the shadows.

"This is Boots who helped Sylvi to find the Gem of Embodiment."

Elin took Boots' hands and looked him in the eye. "I think this one is well on the way to being more than just a friend to our Sylvi."

Boots could feel the blood rush to his cheeks as he gave Sylvi's mother a small nod of the head and looked away.

"But wait," Elin went on, "did you say Sylvi found a healing stone?"

"Yes, mother," said Rania. "That's how you are well again- we found the stones to mend the crown."

Elin's face fell suddenly still.

"The Healing Crown. It worked? This isn't a dream? I've had so many dreams."

She backed up and nearly tripped over a wood Nymph. The North Wind caught her and placed her back on the chaise.

"No, my dear," he said. "You are not dreaming. Your courageous daughters accomplished something the rest of us could not. You are free of your curse."

"I'm free? I'm healed? But it *wasn't* a curse, it was a consequence. I ate the three buds, knowing the price. If the price isn't paid, will my girls... are they safe? You didn't trade *my* health for theirs?"

Elin looked stricken and, indeed, both Rania and Linnea suddenly seemed pale to those around them.

Rania wanted to laugh it off, to tell her mother she was being silly, but a weakness filled her limbs.

She sat on the chaise next to her mother as Linnea put a hand on a table for support.

"The wise woman was afraid of this," said the King. "Quickly, if the crown has healed our Elin, then it can work on the girls as well."

He took the crown from his daughter's head and placed it on Rania as the Queen helped Linnea over to them for her turn.

Boots watched through his tears as they both gained strength. Panic filled his heart for the person who meant more than the world to him. How long would it take to get the crown to the small castle at the northern end of the Westerback forest? "Too long," a voice inside him said, "too long."

43

Home

It didn't take long for the crown to bring a healthy glow back to Rania and Linnea's faces. Boots watched as, one by one, everyone's relief turned to dread.

A hot tear slipped down his face.

"I can get there fastest," said the North Wind.

"No," said Linnea, taking the ring from her finger and bringing it to Boots. "The Troll Castle is your home, is it not?"

Boots pictured hanging laundry as Sylvi told him stories and lunch in the library, searching out clues. He hadn't thought of it in that way before, but the castle really was the only place that had ever felt like a home to him. Mutely, he nodded.

Linnea smiled and took the crown from her head.

"Then this ring will take you there. Bring Sylvi the crown. Make her well."

"And give her this from me," said Rania, catching him in a big bear hug.

"Go quickly," said Elin, "and give her all our love."

"Twist the ring three times and whisper, *home*," said Linnea. "We'll be there as soon as we can."

"And we need to get the stones back to where they belong," said Rania, thinking more of finding a certain quadruped than setting things right.

Boots wiped the tears from his face and didn't waste even a moment in reply before tucking the crown securely under one arm and activating the ring.

He stumbled as his feet hit the ground in the library of the Troll Castle.

"Sylvi!" he yelled, not knowing where to start looking for her. He wasn't sure how long he had been asleep. Surely, she wouldn't still be in the cellar. Would she have gone to her bedroom? It was morning now- would the troll be up and looking for his lingonberry preserves and coffee?

Boots rushed towards the kitchen, yelling her name.

He pelted through the sitting room and almost didn't see the small shape bundled up on the divan.

He rushed to her, banging his knees harshly on the floor.

She looked deathly pale. As he reached out to touch her motionless form, she opened her eyes and smiled weakly.

"I thought you were the troll coming back with herbs," she croaked. "He made me promise I would stay here under the covers until he got back."

Boots smiled at her and brought out the crown. "I hate to say it, but he's wasting his time. Only *this* will do."

Gently, he helped her into a sitting position and placed the crown on her head. The sickly green of her face slowly turned to the vibrant green he had learned to love.

She beamed at him in wonder.

"So, it worked? My mother?"

"Sends her love."

"And my sisters?"

"I'm starting to think you might have exaggerated how horrible they are," he said. "They send you this."

Boots was strangely uncomfortable as he gave Sylvi Rania's hug.

As he pulled away he couldn't help noticing that Sylvi's cheeks were now stained a darker shade of green.

As health came back to her, so did reason. "But, how are you here?" she asked.

He held up his hand, which now had two gold rings on it. "Apparently, princesses can't resist giving me jewelry."

There was a pause before he could make himself go on. "You know, I don't really hate royalty; they're just an easy target. Most of my audiences are poor. They think it's funny. *I* thought it was funny. Can you forgive me?"

Sylvi looked stricken.

"If you can forgive *me* for drugging you with a magic flower and sending you half way round the world."

Boots' brow furrowed. "I know you felt it was the only way," he said, "but next time, could you please just ask?"

"I sincerely hope there is not a 'next time'," she said, "but I can promise you that if I need to drug you with a magical flower in the future, I will ask first. And," she said, biting her lip, "I will let you see my full self- princess and all, from now on."

Boots took her hand and kissed it gently. "Our whole selves. I like that."

He climbed up on the couch next to her, and she put the quilt over his lap. She could feel that the crown had done its work, so she took it off and leaned her head on Boots' shoulder with a sigh.

"I'm glad you're home," she whispered.

"So am I," he said entwining her fingers in his. "So am I."

44

Better than Lemmings

Kai looked at the adorable furry face staring up at him. How had he never noticed how adorable lemmings were? Trapped under his paw with just its face peeking out, the fuzzy little rodent blinked up at him.

"Oh fine," he said, letting the poor thing go. As it scampered away, Kai flopped to the ground. An icy arctic wind ruffled his thick winter coat.

"I knew they couldn't be as delicious as you said they were," laughed a very familiar voice.

Kai jumped up, every fiber of his being electrified.

As he ran to her, Rania dropped to her knees and opened her arms wide. Kai jumped into them and nestled his head into that perfect spot right along her neck. This is where he belonged.

He breathed in deeply and noticed that her smell had changed. He smiled inwardly when he realized it was probably the scent of soap that made the difference.

Another arctic blast nearly knocked them over.

"You're right, Rania, that lake is gorgeous, but I don't think it's worth touching the treasure if it means turning into a lindworm like Uncle Axel."

Kai pulled away to look at the newcomer.

"This is Kai," Rania told her. "I found him!"

"Hi, Kai, I'm Linnea, Rania's sister. She couldn't stop talking about you, so we decided to drop by."

"But," said Kai, "how did you get here? The island is entirely ice-bound. And did you say the lindworm was your *uncle*?"

Before they could answer, an even larger gust crested the hill, and Kai found himself looking up at the mighty North Wind. Kai bowed his head in reverence to the king of the Air Elementals.

"You didn't tell me you were acquainted with the greatest of the Natural Deities," he whispered to Rania.

"There's a lot you don't know about me," she said with a wink. "Care to learn more?"

He did care. He cared an awful lot. "You could start by telling me how your mother is. Did her heroic daughters save the day?"

Rania beamed as she said, "They did, and they are *all* safe now."

"The best of endings," said Kai with his foxy smile. "What's next?"

"We need to finish what our great-great-uncles started," said Rania. "The stones have been removed from the Healing Crown, and we need to return them."

"Sylvi has the Gem of Embodiment," said Linnea. "And we're headed to the Akkan kingdom in the far north to return the Crystal of Cognizance."

"Prince Axel was headed there when he came across the Lindworm treasure," said the North Wind.

"So, the Lindworm really *was* your uncle?" Kai asked Rania.

"My *great, great, great* uncle, but yes. The treasure is enchanted."

"Can we go now?" Linnea asked, tapping a foot on the hard-packed snow.

"Yeah, but not before we stop by the boat sled for a few things," said Rania. "I want to grab the rest of the selkie balm. Traveling by wind is cooold! I also want to see if I can find that sunstone in our gear, and it would be a shame to let the herring jerky go to waste."

"Fine," said Linnea. "But make it quick. I'm worried about Astrid and Pahl."

"Are they the people in Akka who need the crystal?" Kai asked, trying to keep up.

"No," said Linnea. "They are friends from the Southern Continent."

"Astrid's father is the king of Gyldenfare," explained Rania. "He sent a letter to our grandmother saying that Pahl had kidnapped his daughter and his betrothed."

"I am *not* his betrothed!" seethed Linnea.

"Absolutely not," said the North Wind, puffing himself up.

"He and his daughters are traveling to Fullanda," explained Rania.

"And so are Astrid and Pahl," supplied Linnea.

"Pahl, who did *not* kidnap you and Astrid?" Kai guessed.

"Correct," said Linnea in a clipped voice. "Which is why we should get a move on."

The North Wind tried to assure her that the Gusts they sent to warn Astrid and Pahl should have gotten to them already, but Linnea's agitation couldn't be soothed.

"Why don't the two of you go return the crystal," Rania suggested. "Kai and I can sort our gear, and you can pick us up on your way home."

Kai thought the speed at which Linnea and the North Wind left after Rania's suggestion was bordering on rude, but he kept it to himself.

"You know," said Raina as they walked back to the sled, "for a minute there, when I was transported back home, I thought I had broken your enchantment, and you were human again."

Kai held his breath, not knowing if he really wanted to hear how she felt about the idea of him as a human.

"I was so glad that you had been transported with me, but horrified that my actions had caused your change."

Kai breathed again.

"Let's not do that again, ok? – You know, the splitting up part." she said, bumping into him companionably.

"You're stuck with me now, princess," he said, trotting along beside her.

Acknowledgements

This book has gone through many transformations, but it never would have made it to print without the help and support of a lot of amazing people.

-A Tale of Three Cousins-

I come from a family of many wonderful cousins, but this story starts with two in particular: My cousin Chris, who has always inspired me artistically and my cousin Michelle, who always had my back, even when we were driving each other crazy.

When Michelle was diagnosed with stage 4 cancer I started spending a lot of time at her house, helping where I could and giving her space to rest. I wanted to start a writing project I could bring with me, so I asked Chris to choose from some ideas I had been kicking around in my head. At the last minute, I added in the idea of three sisters going on a quest to find magical stones to heal their mother.

My family is a bunch of rock hounds with a history of a hereditary cancer gene, so I probably should have guessed which Chris would select.

As I wrote, Michelle got sicker and her two daughters and I tried to keep things fun, normal and safe. We couldn't give her enchanted sleep or find her magical stones, but we did manage an epic quest to the Minnesota State Fair, where we helped her win prizes and eat things on sticks.

I had seen my own mom go through years of cancer treatment and, miraculously, come through, but sometimes it doesn't matter how hard you fight or believe. Sometimes cancer is just too big.

This book is dedicated to all those family, friends and care-givers who bear witness to their loved one's pain and wish they could do more.

Illness is hard, no matter what side of it you are on. Be kind to yourselves.

-Tack Så Mycket!-

To my grandparents who took me hunting for agates and gnome homes in the woods surrounding their cabin. The stories and traditions they brought with them from the 'old country' fueled my love of Nordic culture and the authors and artists that inspired the kingdoms of Sarnmark: Peter Christen Asbjørnsen, Jørgen Moe, John Bauer, Astrid Lindgren, Selma Lagerlöf, Kay Nielsen, Snorri Sturluson & Elias Lönnrot.

Another big Tack goes out to the American Swedish Institute (ASI) & Ingella Ellert Haaland for the continuing education course, Scandinavian Myths.

-Many, Many Thanks!-

I am lucky enough to be part of two wonderfully supportive and inspiring writing groups. A good portion of this book was written or made better at their meetings and retreats.

Thank you Sarah, Stella, Chris, Lawrence & Zach and all of the amazing folks in the Laini Taylor Patreon crew. You guys are the best!

Tremendous thanks always go out to Laura Piotrowski for being my first reader/editor, for believing in my work like no one else and for giving me the courage to move forward.

Many grateful thanks to the talented folks at NYDB, particularly Stella Brown, who worked hard to make this beautiful object you hold in your hands, and Robert Stevens who created the beautiful map of Sarnmark. Thank you for trusting my vision while helping me to push further.

To all the people who read the Kindle Vella version, one episode a week for over a year (particularly Rorie, who always let me know whenever she loved something).

To Joann for all you do and for all the extra help you gave so that I could get this done.

To my parents, for supporting my crazy endeavors- from skits in the backyard to novel writing. We've been through a lot (hugs & smooches).

To Hattie & Jaana, for all the walks, talks and coffee.

To Matthew & Henry- You guys are awesome. I feel so lucky to be your mom.

To Malin & Peyton- For making art and slime in the kitchen and all the crazy times together. I am so grateful to have you in my life.

And to Tony- for all the stuffs & for teaching me to believe in happy endings, again. I love you!

Emily K. Stevens

Emily is an author, illustrator and surface designer
who grew up on the shores of Lake Superior. Her
works include Adam Larson, Master of Disguise,
The Legend of Poopman and Drama Diaries,
written with Sadie Graham. Emily currently lives in
Minnesota with her husband and two kids.

Learn more at emilykstevens.com

www.ingramcontent.com/pod-product-compliance
Lightning Source LLC
Chambersburg PA
CBHW061953170626

46813CB00006B/2633